"What's wrong, Amber? Did I say something to hurt you?"

"Of course not." She shook her head. "Let's go."

Luke held on to her upper arms and searched her face as if her reason for her meltdown was inked on her face.

It would be so easy to step into his arms, just to lay her head on his chest for a while or get a warm hug.

Instead, Luke gently held her face in his hands and kissed her forehead. It was so tender, she almost cried again.

"I hate it when women cry, especially you, Amber. You're such a strong woman—something must be really bothering you."

"I can't tell you. Not right now, Luke. I will someday if the occasion presents itself."

He bent his head and kissed her lips—softly, lightly. "I'll wait until you're ready."

When he stopped, she wanted to scream. Then his lips closed over hers again, and it was just like her dreams, only much, much better. With each kiss, she knew that she'd never be the same again.

Dear Reader,

Welcome to Beaumont, Oklahoma, the home of the three bull-riding Beaumont brothers: Luke, Reed and Jesse. They are all Gold Buckle Cowboys.

Luke Beaumont's story begins my "bull-riding Beaumont brothers" trilogy, which I hope you'll enjoy.

Of course, Luke is a sexy bull rider (is there any other kind?) who ignored Sergeant Amber Chapman throughout high school. But then she arrives at a public autograph session and gives him a piece of her mind. A big piece. Luke is a prize-winning cowboy who has some personal items to deal with, including Amber Chapman. Lots of luck, Luke!

Life is also good in Central New York, where I live, but I'm writing this in sunny Florida in our new motor home. We plan on driving to some PBR events as well as visiting some rodeos.

See you there!

Chris Wenger

THE COWBOY AND THE COP

———

CHRISTINE WENGER

HARLEQUIN® WESTERN ROMANCE

Recycling programs
for this product may
not exist in your area.

ISBN-13: 978-0-373-75776-3

The Cowboy and the Cop

Copyright © 2017 by Christine Wenger

Printed in U.S.A.

www.Harlequin.com

Christine Wenger has worked in the criminal justice field for more years than she cares to remember, but now spends her time reading, writing and seeing the sights in our beautiful world. A native Central New Yorker, she loves watching professional bull riding and rodeo with her favorite cowboy, her husband, Jim. You can reach Chris at PO Box 1823, Cicero, NY 13039, or through her website at christinewenger.com.

To all cowboys and cops,

Be careful out there!

And to Michele Goldstein, new friend,
who keeps smiling through every challenge.
Chocolate will help!

Chapter One

What am I doing here? I feel like a buckle bunny.

Several times Amber Chapman thought of leaving the Professional Bull Riders autograph session in the huge Oklahoma City arena. She'd stood in bull rider Luke Beaumont's line way too long so she could give him a piece of her mind.

I have a million things to do back home.

Maybe she should just let the three Beaumont brothers find out on their own that they were going to lose the ranch that had been in their family for generations, but she just couldn't do that to the brothers, not even Luke, no matter how much she disliked him. Besides, their town would suffer the most, since the Beaumont Ranch employed many of the locals…or at least it used to.

Not anymore. Not in its present state.

Luke barely looked up at her when Amber finally stood in front of him. Robotically he slid over a glossy eight-by-ten picture of himself.

"Who would you like me to sign it to?" he said, a black felt-tip pen poised over a large photo of him riding a huge bull.

"Sergeant Amber Chapman of Beaumont, Oklahoma, but actually you can skip the autograph and the photo."

Luke looked up from his place at the long table of bull riders signing and posing for pictures with their fans.

He grinned. "Amber? Amber Chapman. Hey, it's been a long time. I didn't know you were a fan."

She had forgotten that he had the brightest blue eyes—more like turquoise. The lights of the arena made them even bluer.

Amber noticed, of course, but she didn't care. She wasn't there to look at his eyes or at how his muscles stretched out his chambray shirt, or how good he smelled. Like leather and pine.

She refocused on the task at hand. Placing her hands on the table, Amber leaned over so only he could hear.

"There're a couple of things I need to make you aware of, Luke, but I'm not going to go into them now. There are too many people within hearing distance, and you have a long line waiting. What I have to say is for your ears only. You can fill your brothers in later."

She looked down the long parade of tables. She spotted the other two Beaumonts: Reed and Jesse, Luke's younger brothers.

Amber whispered, "I saw a bar across the street from the stadium. It's called the Silver Spur. I'll meet you there. And, by the way, I'm not a fan of yours."

Okay, that was a lie. He was a good rider who'd probably win the Finals. Besides, he was a hometown celebrity and that brought a lot of attention to the town of Beaumont.

"And here I was hoping you waited in line for my autograph and a selfie." Luke grinned. "Are you still mad at me over the senior prom?"

Yeah, she was still mad at him. It seemed ridiculous to hold a grudge for so long, but there was only one senior prom in her lifetime, and it had been the worst night of her life.

"I'm not here to talk about that, and don't flatter yourself, Luke. I'm not one of your groupies." She rolled her eyes. "And why would you think I was?"

"Because you had to drive here from Beaumont. Let's see…Beaumont to Oklahoma City…that's more than a three-hour drive."

"I like to drive. I like bull riding in general."

"But you still haven't forgiven me, huh?"

"Not particularly. How am I supposed to forgive you when you ruined one of the most important events of senior year by getting my date drunk and sending him home in a taxi?"

"He was a jerk."

"He was my date. Maybe someone should have had the courtesy of telling me where he was."

"I should have told you right away. I admit it. Can we just forget about it?"

"I suppose it was a long time ago. I can think about forgiving you."

He raised a perfect black eyebrow. "Well, at least you asked me out to a bar. That's a start."

Amber gritted her teeth. "I need to talk to you, that's all. No more."

"It must be really important."

"Of course it's important. Or why would I have driven all this way? Oh, and by the way, when the Beaumonts are champions of our hometown again, Luke, then you can autograph a picture for me and we can take a selfie. Just meet me after this circus so we can talk."

Luke Beaumont scanned the packed bar for Amber. It seemed that the entire arena had emptied out and gathered into a two-thousand-square-foot building. People were packed elbow to elbow; most sported denim and clutched a beer in their hand.

The dance floor was equally full. Patrons were dancing in between tables, some *on* the tables.

The Silver Spur wasn't the quiet spot that Amber wanted.

Suddenly applause started—low at first then it picked up steam. Everyone turned to look at him. Cheers resounded through the room.

"Yeah, Luke!"

"Congratulations, Luke!"

"Yeehaw!"

He didn't particularly like the attention. Yes, he'd won the PBR event tonight, but there were a lot of other bull riders who deserved applause for great rides. He'd just got lucky.

Luke tipped his hat to the crowd and they went back to what they'd been doing. No one approached him for autographs or selfies, but a waitress came over with a frosty longneck and a stack of bar tokens toward drinks.

Sweet.

Finally he saw Amber waving to him.

The crowd parted as he zigzagged toward her, but he had to run a gauntlet of handshakes, backslaps and flirty smiles along with pieces of paper slipped into his shirt pocket. Phone numbers.

He'd never called one of the numbers given to him. Never.

He tipped his hat to Amber, slid into a chair opposite her and pulled out his stack of tokens. "Can I buy you a drink?"

"I'll have a ginger ale. I have to drive home tonight."

All he had to do was hold up his hand and a waitress was at his side.

"A ginger ale for the lady and I'll take another one of these." He pointed to his bottle.

While he waited for Amber to tell him what was on her mind, he leaned back on his chair and wondered why she looked so different to him. He'd seen her around town occasionally, but he'd never really looked at her. She was just there, like most of Beaumont. He knew just about everyone casually and had gone to school with a good chunk of the population—after all it was a small town—but he didn't really know Amber.

He'd seen her in a sheriff's uniform once and that had surprised him. Her father and brothers weren't exactly pillars of the community. They tried just about every get-rich-quick scheme known to mankind, and their junkyard was known for hot car parts. And their moonshine…well, when the word got around that a new batch was ready, there was usually a line at the junkyard's back door.

Their drinks were delivered along with more tokens. Still, he waited for her to tell him what was on her mind.

After the waitress left, Amber crossed her arms and leaned toward him. Her usually full lips were clasped together in a thin, white line, but her eyes were the greenest of green, like emeralds. Her shoulder-length hair had various shades of blond, and she wasn't loaded with makeup, but those emerald eyes began to narrow.

This wasn't going to be good.

"Luke, have you been home lately?"

"If you follow the PBR, you know I haven't. Every weekend, there's another event. I'm on the tour and close to winning the season. If you're worried about us seeing my father, we got him a cell phone and call him a lot.

He knows that I can't be around much. The same with my brothers."

"Isn't there a summer break coming up soon?"

"Yep. After Billings, Montana, this weekend."

"As you recently told me, you are only three hours from home."

"I know, but I might as well be in Alaska. I have way too many things I have to do right now and the week after Billings."

"You'd better change your plans and the sooner the better," Amber said.

"Why, what's going on?"

She pulled out a piece of paper from her purse, unfolded it and handed it to him. "It's a copy. Your ranch is going up for auction for back taxes in two weeks."

He scanned the letter. "Dammit!"

"Big Dan didn't tell you?" she asked.

"Of course not. My father doesn't care about the ranch. Not since my mother died." Looking at the letter again, he shook his head. "And that's when my father stopped paying taxes. I know he doesn't give a hoot about the ranch anymore, but I thought he was at least keeping up with the taxes. We've been sending him money..."

He shrugged.

"It's easy to see that Big Dan hasn't been putting money into the ranch, Luke. It's been a mess since Hurricane Daphne. Your outbuildings are falling down, the main barn's roof has a hole in it, and the handful of stock your father didn't sell is scattered to the wind. Your neighbors and former workers took them in and have been taking care of them. The homestead's portico is hanging on by one post and some windows are blown out. My brothers boarded them up."

A plan was already formulating in his mind but he had to get Jesse and Reed, his brothers, involved. The Beaumont Ranch had been part of their heritage since the late nineteenth century land rush in Oklahoma. Old Pierre Beaumont might have been a "Sooner," someone who jumped the whistle too soon, but he'd plopped his wagon on acres of prime cattle and horse land. Throughout the decades, his descendants had added a total of twenty-thousand acres to the original homestead.

"I promise that I'll get home in two weeks, and take care of things," he said.

"That'll be cutting it close, but you'll make the auction."

"You mean I can't buy it back before then? I could send a check."

"It's too late for that." She shook her head. "And that'd have to be one big check."

"Did my father get notices?"

"Of course he did. I happen to know that Connie McBride, who runs the tax department, personally delivered several notices to him."

He took a long draw of his beer. "This is just getting worse and worse by the second. But you drove all that way, watched the bull riding, stood in my autographing line. Why did you put yourself out? I mean, we've barely seen each other since high school. Why are you helping us?"

"Because the Beaumont Ranch employs a good chunk of the town, and the town is suffering, Luke. The homestead used to be a tourist attraction, which added to our economy. It's on the list of national historic places, for heaven's sake. Now the high school kids are using it for partying at night."

"I didn't know, but thanks for telling me."

"Don't thank me yet." Amber held up a hand to stop him. "Hang on, there's more. Much more, and it gets way worse."

Luke had a sickening feeling in the pit of his stomach. What could be worse? Any adrenaline left over from his win was quickly vanishing.

"You might not know, but I'm a sergeant with the Beaumont County Sheriff's Department. I arrested your father three times."

"Arrested Big Dan? Three times?" His voice grew loud then he lowered it. "What the hell did he do?"

"Bar fights. Big Dan is turning into the town drunk, Luke. And he's a shadow of his former self," Amber said softly. "He's wasting away. But with any luck, his probation officer, Matty Matthews, and inpatient rehab will help him."

He tapped his fingers on the table to get rid of some nervous energy. "I know Matty. We were in junior rodeo together. But probation? And inpatient rehab?" Luke sat back in his chair. "I can't picture my father being successful at either."

"I'll tell you more about it when you come home. I really should be leaving soon. I have an early shift in the morning."

"Listen, Amber." Luke sighed. "I don't know why I'm telling you this but, truth be told, I've been avoiding going home. In that way, I'm a lot like my father. And sometimes I feel like I've lost both parents. So I threw myself into bull riding to forget everything."

Amber made a move to put her hand over his, but clearly changed her mind at the last minute and took a sip of her ginger ale instead.

"I really should get going, Luke."

"Thanks for making it a point to tell me everything. I really appreciate it. So will my brothers. If we lost the ranch, well…it'd be a tough blow. Let me walk you to your car."

They walked to the lot near the arena in silence. "Here is mine." She pointed. "The red Honda SUV."

He waited as she opened the door. "Well, see you at home, Luke."

"Give me a week after Billings. I'll get right on a plane and will land at the auction."

She smiled.

It didn't seem like Amber smiled often; she was very serious. Then again, she'd had some very serious things to tell him.

He'd opened up to her and couldn't figure out why. He'd never told anyone what he'd just told her.

But Amber had changed. In high school, she was quiet and had ten-foot walls around her that only the brave—or stupid—would approach. She hadn't had many friends, mostly due to her family's moonshining activities and rumors of them selling hot car parts. The fact that she lived in a fairly dilapidated house surrounded by a junkyard made her the brunt of even more hurtful comments.

He'd always quelled those kind of jokes, because he'd seen the sadness in her eyes, the tightness of her lips. He'd seen her hurry away for the protection of a dark corner, and then he'd seen her cry.

Why hadn't he done more to stop the jokes? Instead, he'd only succeeded in his classmates not joking about her in front of him, but he knew that it still occurred.

He should have done more back then to help her, and

now Amber had given him the biggest gift of his life by telling him about his ranch.

"See you at home, Luke."

He took her hand and couldn't decide whether to shake it or kiss the back of it. So he pulled her toward him in a hug and kissed her forehead.

He heard her slight gasp and he smiled.

She was smiling, too.

There was a little crack in that wall around her and he wondered if he could knock it down for good and get to know more of Deputy Sheriff Sergeant Amber Chapman.

Chapter Two

"Six…seven…eight! He did it, ladies and gentlemen! He did it!"

The announcer's voice echoed through the cavernous arena in Billings.

Luke did a flying dismount from his bull, Cowabunga. Then the animal pushed him with his huge nose across the arena dirt as if Luke was a rolling pin. Luke felt that the bull actually knew he'd beaten him. That was Cowabunga's revenge.

Every bone in his body screamed and his teeth rattled in his head. He knew he had whacked his knee again. It took all the effort he could muster to get up, run to the chute gate and climb to safety until the bullfighters got the massive bull out of the arena and into his pen.

"The winner of the Iron Cowboy Showdown is none other than Luke Beaumont!" Dwight Frenza, the arena announcer, said enthusiastically.

Luke knew the drill. When Dwight said, "Everyone put your hands together for the winner…" it was Luke's signal to stand in front of the Professional Bull Riders sign and be interviewed and presented with a gold buckle and maybe a new pair of boots.

The big check would come later.

Good. He needed it.

Behind the chutes, several monitors were set up and he stopped to see the updated stats. Between the slaps on his back and hearty handshakes from other riders and PBR personnel congratulating him, Luke noticed that his two brothers had dropped a couple places on the standings, but he had no doubt that his brothers would move up. Out of the top twenty-five professional riders, he was number one. Reed was now fourth and Jesse was fifth. Together they were known as the Beaumont Big Guns.

Speaking of Reed and Jesse, both came bounding out of the locker room. Reed had a bag of ice taped to his shoulder and a black eye. Jesse had a bandage around his right hand and wrist.

Reed pumped his hand. "Incredible ride, bro."

Jesse gave him a fist bump with his good hand. "You did it again, Luke! Three wins in a row."

"Everyone fairly okay?" Luke asked.

"Just a little nick from my last bull's horns," Reed said.

"Nothing worth mentioning." Jesse shrugged. "But how are you doing, Luke? You took quite a rolling from Cowabunga."

"I think I trashed my knee again. It hurts like hell. I'll head to Sports Medicine. They'll probably tape it and remind me again to get surgery."

"Don't forget the autographing, Luke. As usual, the fans will be lined up to see you," Reed said.

Luke looked forward to signings because he loved talking to fans of the sport. Once in a while, someone from his past would go through his line and it was cool to get reacquainted.

Just like Amber Chapman. But they really hadn't gotten reacquainted. She'd sternly pointed out that he'd better take care of the ranch and the town or both would disintegrate.

Amber had looked good. Her shoulder-length hair was various shades of blond and her green eyes had looked like new spring grass. He didn't know why he was being poetic when he thought of Amber. He must have been bucked off too many times and smacked his head.

He'd thought about what Amber had told him for the entire week before the Billings event, but what he hadn't done was talk to his brothers. He'd wanted to do that in person, and now was the time.

Their Oklahoma roots went back to about 1836 when their great-great-grandfather, Pierre Beaumont, rode from Gonzales, Texas, to fight for the Alamo and stayed to establish a town and a ranch on the outskirts of San Antonio that he called Beaumont.

Although there had been several Beaumonts who'd run the ranch, expanded it and cared for it like Pierre, Big Dan hadn't given a hoot about anything since his lovely wife, Valerie Lynn O'Malley Beaumont, had died in his arms after being kicked in the head by a horse.

Big Dan had easily fallen into booze and gambling, and resorted to yelling at his sons when they came to visit. He insisted that he didn't want the ranch touched. Instead he wanted it frozen in time—the time that Valerie died.

Luke waved his brothers over to a corner of the locker room. "I have to talk to you both. There's a great steakhouse down the street. It's called Old Barn or something like that. After the autographing, let's grab some steaks and talk."

"Anything important?" Reed asked.

"I think it is."

LATER THAT NIGHT the three Beaumont Big Guns were treated like celebrities at the Old Barn. Over thick, rare steaks and curly fries with brown gravy, they posed for pictures, signed various pieces of clothing and several programs from the event.

"You are so handsome, Luke, and the best rider—ever," a much-too-young girl said with her hand on his arm. "Reed is the brainiac, and Jesse is the party guy, but you're...uh...like both of them, and you're the best. I have your poster over my bed."

As he removed her hand, he was amazed that she had his two brothers nailed perfectly. And he...well, she wasn't the first fan who'd commented on his looks. As for being the best rider ever, he could think of many who were much better. He was just lucky enough to be on top right now. It could change at any minute.

Actually it was going to change soon. He wasn't going to ride in other circuits over PBR's summer break. He was going home for a while before Amber Chapman handcuffed him and dragged him home.

During a quiet moment, Luke turned to his brothers. "Hey, I want to talk to you about the ranch. It's going on the auction block for back taxes in one week. Dad hasn't paid the taxes since Mom died."

"But we sent him money," Reed said.

Luke sighed. "Obviously, he drank it away."

Reed took a draw on his beer. "Three years is a lot of back taxes."

"How do you know all this?" Jesse asked.

"I talked to Amber Chapman—or rather, she talked to me and let me have it. You remember Amber. Now she's a deputy sheriff, and said she's arrested Dad three times.

The third time he got probation and is in rehab right now. His probation officer is Matty Matthews."

"No kidding," Jesse said in disbelief.

Reed grunted. "Dad's on probation? And sitting in rehab? Knowing how he has been acting since Mom died, he isn't going to last long at either one. I know Matty Matthews and he's not going to take any crap from Dad. Big Dan will soon be in big-boy prison and doing big-boy time."

Luke leaned forward. "We could pay off the taxes. There's one week before the auction. If you guys are going to keep riding, I'll go home and bid on it. During the summer, I'll get things repaired and fixed up."

The three brothers sat in silence until Jesse spoke.

"It's all hard to take, but remember when we were kids, we constantly played Musketeers. Remember our oath?"

Jesse put his right hand in the middle of the table, palm down. Reed grinned and put his on top of his younger brother's. Luke put his hand on top of the stack.

"One for all and all for one!" the Beaumont brothers vowed.

"Good." Luke knew his brothers would come through. "I'm glad you feel the same as I do. Mom wouldn't have wanted the ranch to fall into ruin. When Dad snaps out of his funk, he'll realize that he almost lost the whole enchilada. Maybe he'll care then, maybe not."

Luke continued. "We'll have to pool our resources for the auction, and it might take a huge chunk of change, especially if other people bid, too. Luckily, we're all riding great and winning at the present moment." Luke chuckled. "I have a bunch of commitments that I can't escape during the next several days—pictures for some calendar and a jeans commercial. But I'll be at the auction—I promise—and I'll be in touch with more information."

Jesse nodded. "Looks like Reed and I will be picking up another circuit for the summer to keep the money coming in. Okay with you, bro?"

Reed took a draw on his beer. "No sweat. We'll ride in Tucson."

Luke got up from the table. "We need some wins, brothers, so good luck. The ranch is going to take a lot of the green stuff."

"Don't forget the check, Mr. Gold Buckle." Reed picked up the bill and handed it to Luke. "You know our rule—winner pays."

"Yeah, cowboy. You make the big bucks," Jesse added.

Since his brothers hadn't hesitated to pitch in to get the ranch back in shape, Luke was never so happy to pay a check and take their kidding.

Now, if only things would go as well with Big Dan Beaumont.

THE TOWN OF Beaumont was unusually free of calls for a Monday morning, so Amber pulled out her study guide for the state police exam and went through the questions that she'd missed before. Opening a notebook, she jotted down some key words. She'd look up what she'd gotten wrong, make notes and study those for the future.

But even with a perfect score, Amber knew the biggest obstacle still was ahead, namely the background check. Even though her father claimed that his used car parts business was on the up-and-up, Amber could never be sure. And, if the officials found anything questionable, Amber would find herself stuck here in a town that still looked at her as Marv Chapman's kid.

She'd tried to believe her father when he'd said they'd all be crime-free while she was a deputy sheriff and that no "funny business" would be going on, but could she trust him?

She was already a traitor in her father's and three brothers' eyes because she had gone "over to the other side." They were mostly kidding when they teased her—mostly.

The residents of Beaumont looked down on the Chapmans and always would. But her goal for the longest time was to bring some respectability to the family name. That's one of the reasons why she'd become a cop. The other was to keep her father and brothers in line. So far, so good, on that count.

Her mother had been looking for the same respectability. Kathleen Chapman had stayed with her husband and sons and tolerated their minor brushes with the law until Amber was accepted into college. Then Kathleen had taken a job in the cafeteria at the University of Oklahoma and the two of them had shared a small apartment.

Those were some of Amber's happiest times.

And although they'd never divorced, Kathleen still had a soft spot for Marv and her three boys who followed in Marv's footsteps: Aaron, Kyle and Ronnie.

There was some kind of loud commotion in the hallway. Amber was just about to lay her study guide down and check it out, when the door opened and a man—or rather, a cowboy—walked in.

He wore the typical dress of every other cowboy in town: jeans, a long-sleeved shirt, a dinner plate of a buckle, a hat and dusty boots.

Leaning over the counter, he raised an eyebrow

when he saw that Amber was holding a study guide. She quickly closed it and tossed it into her desk drawer.

"Hello, Luke. You made it."

"If I'm not disturbing you—"

"You're not disturbing me. Although the noise in the hallway did. Was that your fan club?"

"Uh…just some people who were congratulating me on my wins in Billings and Oklahoma City."

"Let me add my congratulations."

"Thanks, Amber." He took a deep breath and looked down at the marble floor. Finally he asked, "How about filling me in on my father's arrests?"

Amber pulled a folder from her bottom drawer and opened it. Although she knew its contents by heart, Luke Beaumont always made her jumpy, and it gave her something to do with her hands.

"I think I told you that I arrested him three times. They were all at Tommy Lang's bar. For the first two arrests I recommended to Judge Bascom that he just give him a stern warning and tell him to go to AA, but not the third time. That time, I recommended some days in jail along with probation and inpatient rehab. Your dad's a fighter when he's drunk and he can get quite mean, especially if someone brings up your mom."

Luke grunted. "I'm sure he's more miserable than ever, but tell me what he did at the bar. Obviously he was drunk. Any damage?"

"Yeah. The last time he jumped a biker who called him an old drunk. Your father said that he might be a drunk, but he wasn't old. More words were exchanged relative to size and stature, and when the peanut shells settled on the floor, the damage totaled one thousand bucks."

"I'll pay it."

"Your father is supposed to pay his own restitution," Amber instructed.

"Yeah, well, my money is going to have to do."

"That'll teach him," she mumbled.

"Where's the tax department? I have an appointment to see Connie McBride."

"There's a sign right next to the entranceway, but your fans were probably blocking your view," she teased. "It's on the second floor. Up the stairs, turn left. Sign on door."

"Thank you, Sergeant Chapman."

Her heart was pounding in her chest. Why did he have to be so hot?

"I'll leave you alone now, so you can get back to your reading. I'm glad Beaumont is crime-free, except for our fathers, huh? State police study guide?"

She wanted to coat him with pepper spray from the top of his Stetson to the bottom of his boots.

"If you want to pay your father's restitution, so he wouldn't have learned a thing from his experience, you can do so on the third floor in the Beaumont County Probation Department. Do you want me to draw you a map?" she said, trying to get back at his teasing her.

"I can handle it. Riding bulls hasn't scrambled my brains that much."

She grinned. "The jury is still out on that, Luke."

He touched the brim of his hat to her. "Maybe I'll stop in and see Matty Matthews while I'm there."

As he walked toward the thick oak door and opened it, Amber couldn't help but notice his tight butt.

That cowboy can really work a pair of jeans.

She could hear his boots knocking on the marble floor until they faded.

Sergeant Chapman hurried to the refrigerator in the break room, opened the freezer and let the air cool her flaming face.

Chapter Three

Amber looked great in the navy blue and white Beaumont County Sheriff's Department uniform with full cop regalia, but Luke still remembered her at the senior prom, all sparkly and glowing. Crazy Kenny Fowler had been her date and he'd paid more attention to everyone but Amber.

During the prom, Luke got word that Kenny had Chapman moonshine on him and even more jars of the stuff in his car that he got "on sale" for taking Amber to the prom.

Luke had known exactly when Amber had heard Crazy Kenny say that stupid sentence. With head held high, she'd left. He'd excused himself from his date and secretly followed Amber home, just to make sure she'd gotten there all right.

He couldn't help but hear her soft sobs as she'd slipped out of her heels on the sidewalk and kept on walking.

Funny, he remembered Amber that evening but he couldn't remember whom he'd taken to the prom.

Reaching the second floor, he found the door labeled Beaumont County Department of Taxation and walked in. The office smelled musty, as if fresh air had never hit all the ledgers, microfiche and file cabinets. Looked like the tax department hadn't caught up to the digital age.

"I know why you're here, Luke," said Mrs. McBride from behind the counter. Connie McBride was the mother of Leann, the head cheerleader he had dated during his sophomore year. "I've been expecting you."

Reaching to her right, she slid a file from the top of the stack and positioned it in front of him. Using a stubby index finger with a nail cut to the quick, she pointed to a figure he knew was reachable but would be painful for his brothers and him.

"And these are the penalties." She pointed to another figure.

Dammit, Dad. What have you done?

"I had no idea it was so much," Luke mumbled.

"As I told you on the phone, according to the rules, I have no choice but to put your property up for auction," Mrs. McBride leaned over the counter. "Hopefully, no one else will bid on it and you can buy it back. It has to go for at least these two figures. That's the bottom line. The sale starts at ten o'clock sharp, Luke." She checked her watch. "It's nine thirty now. I'd better get going."

"Is it downstairs?" Luke asked.

"No. It's in the lobby of the courthouse. Not here."

How could he be so stupid? He took her hand and shook it. "Thanks, Mrs. McBride. Oh, and how's Leann?"

"She's just a saint. She's married and living in Fargo with an immature husband and four hellion boys—two sets of twins. I don't know how she does it."

He tipped his hat. "Thanks, Mrs. McBride." He'd have to pay his father's restitution for the three bar fights at a later date.

As he walked, he phoned Reed and told him the total amount. "Good. We're covered and there's some left," Reed said.

"Is Jesse with you?" Luke asked.

"Yeah. I'll put you on speakerphone so he can hear. We're in Tucson now, chowing down on some cold pizza for breakfast and sitting outside on the balcony of our hotel."

"Someone could outbid me, but I still think I have it covered," Luke advised. His heart beat fast in his chest. A lot was at stake. Not only now, but for future generations of Beaumonts. The ranch was a living history of his family, and it made him get both misty and mad that his father had forgotten that. "Thanks, guys. I'd better get moving. I'll talk to you later."

"Good luck with Dad, bro," Jesse said. "He was ornery and stubborn the last time I visited with him at the ranch. Not a lot of fun."

"He's really going to blow when he finds out that we're going to save the ranch," Reed added.

A sick feeling came over Luke, when he thought about the ranch. It used to be prosperous and whatever his father touched had turned to profit. They'd been noted for their rough stock far and wide.

But Big Dan had given away all the stock—bulls, horses, everything. The first to go was the horse that had kicked his mother in the head.

Erasing all memories of his thriving ranch was how his father had grieved. This devastated the brothers, who couldn't stop Big Dan, so they threw themselves into riding bulls and staying away from the ranch and their father.

In retrospect, the whole bunch of them should have gone to counseling.

"Jesse, it's time for you to win," Luke said, shaking off what he still didn't want to deal with.

"No kidding," Jesse said.

They said their goodbyes and Luke disconnected.

As he walked to the courthouse he thought he'd rather ride a two-thousand-pound, bucking Brahma bull with horns as big as baseball bats than deal with his father.

"SERGEANT CHAPMAN, I'm assigning you to the tax auction. Crowd control. Then you need to direct traffic when it's over," Captain Fred Fitzgerald informed her.

Amber hated working tax auctions, but as Captain Fitz had said previously, "Someone has to keep all of them from killing Connie McBride, and I outrank you."

She was always that someone.

As the only woman on the small force, Captain Fitzgerald gave her the assignments that none of the men wanted, or the ones that Fitz felt were beneath his macho deputies, and that made her feel frustrated and angry. She'd tried talking to Fitz on several occasions, and he'd always insisted that he was treating her the same as the other officers, so she got nowhere.

A larger force with more opportunities for advancement was one of many reasons why Amber wanted to get into the state police. Although there were probably Fitz types in the state police, there were more departments to transfer into if she got a Fitz.

When they offered a state police exam, she'd have to pass that, be reachable on the list, submit to a background check and several interviews along with the agility test.

Agility test. Ugh. She couldn't get much agility sitting behind a desk. She jogged, of course, but she really should work out more. Maybe with a punching bag.

She vowed to join Marco's Fit-nasium. It was the only gym in town.

Connie McBride was her usual busy self. Thank goodness she had an auctioneer who was going to do the actual sale of the property. Connie would faint if she had to do that chatter.

Bidders had been lined up since dawn and they were loud. They complained about everything like death, taxes and how rock-and-roll singers were taking over traditional country music, but mostly about taxes.

Luke Beaumont was in the crowd. She saw him leaning against the beige marble wall, a couple of fingers through the loops of his jeans. She couldn't tell if he was amused or irritated, but he kept looking at the clock. Nine thirty-five.

Less than a half hour to go.

Amber didn't think anyone in Beaumont could outbid him if Luke had the money, but there were always out-of-town speculators and condo builders looking for big chunks of land like the Beaumont property.

Amber walked toward Luke. When he saw her, he tweaked the brim of his hat. She liked it when guys did that. It was very gentlemanly.

"Having fun?" she asked.

"Oh, yeah."

"Now you know how your fans feel when they are waiting in line for your autograph."

"I've always known how they felt," Luke said. "And I appreciate every one of them."

She was just about to tell him that on several occasions she'd been one of those fans waiting in line for him, but always changed her mind at the last minute—except for the time that had brought him here.

Amber looked around. "I recognize a couple of men who have traditionally bought up property at auction.

Be ready, Luke. And I hope you have a lot of money in reserve."

"Between my brothers and me, we ought to win the bid. And, Amber, thanks for coming to Oklahoma City and letting me know about…everything. I appreciate that you gave me a wake-up call."

She shrugged her shoulders. She was only helping an old high school friend. That was all. Right?

"Good luck, Luke."

"Thanks."

Amber told herself that she just wanted to keep Beaumont the way it was—a nice, small town with lots of scenic grazing land dotted with cattle, horses and sheep and no absentee landlords.

It had nothing to do with the fact that Luke Beaumont was always traveling. Now he had to stay home for a relatively long period of time.

Not that she'd notice.

Moving to the back of the room, Amber eavesdropped on three men she didn't recognize. They were looking at a survey map. She was almost certain it was the plot of the Beaumont Ranch. When she got an opportunity to peek, her suspicions were confirmed.

Luke had better be ready with buckets of money.

Everyone knew that he was a star with the Professional Bull Riders, and had made a lot of money riding with them. She also knew that he'd had a lot of injuries and that medical insurance for PBR riders, if anyone *would* insure them, was astronomical. She'd bet that Luke had a lot of medical bills that he had to pay.

Amber looked at the sign-in sheet which showed the times that everyone signed in. Perfect! The three strangers were last to sign in.

Amber Chapman made a split decision to help Luke.

Because she didn't want him to feel indebted to her, she hoped he'd never find out.

After all, she was only doing her job.

IN THE LOBBY of the courthouse, the auctioneer pounded his gavel on the makeshift podium—a dark gray metal desk that had big rust spots on three sides.

"Now we have the Beaumont Ranch, which consists of a four-thousand-square-foot historic ranch house, several barns, several outbuildings and over twenty thousand acres of prime land. You all have the information—now let's get started."

Suddenly, Amber Chapman's voice rang out. "Attention, please. Attention! We are over capacity in the lobby. I'm sorry, but I have to ask the following individuals to step out. You were the last to sign in, and because of our fire rules, you have to be the first to leave. The individuals are Mark McGee, Dave Hartman, Jr., and Ray Maldonado. Please step outside, gentlemen."

"Are you serious?" said one of them.

"I am," Amber replied.

"But we are going to bid on the Beaumont property," said a stocky, bald man. His face was flushed.

Luke heard him say that loud and clear. Thank goodness the three men had to leave. Interesting—Luke never thought that the Beaumont Sheriff's Department was a stickler on details, like kicking three guys out due to the fire rules, but it was to his benefit.

"Please step outside, gentlemen, and we'll discuss the matter. Just as soon as another three people leave the facility, I can let you three back in."

She held the door open for the three to pass.

"We could care less about any other property, Sergeant. We'll be leaving this jerkwater town," one of them said. "And for the record, Beaumont's rule about having to be present to bid is medieval. We could have sent a proxy and not wasted our time."

Amber was glad that Beaumont had that rule, or all types of speculators hoping to grab up property would descend on their tax auctions. Of course, they could sell the property at any time to whomever they wanted, but Beaumont's rule added just one more level of making things a little more difficult for out-of-town bidders.

As soon as the last one cleared the door, Amber closed it and stood against it. "Sorry for the interruption, Mr. Auctioneer. Please proceed," Amber yelled over the noise of the crowd.

"Thank you, Sergeant Chapman. Now, let's start the bidding, folks."

When the dust settled, Luke Beaumont and his brothers owned the Beaumont Ranch, or whatever was left of it.

That hadn't been his plan. He was just going to pay the back taxes. That's all. It'd still be in his father's name.

But not now.

According to county rules and regulations, because he had the winning bid, he owned the Beaumont Ranch.

Since his brothers had pitched in their fair share, sooner or later he'd have to put the deed in their names, too.

He felt elated and relieved. The ranch had almost slipped through his fingers, but it was back. It was a close call, but, thanks to Amber, there was a positive outcome. Luke was thrilled that he and his brothers were able to preserve and protect his family's legacy.

Later, Luke would have to tell Big Dan that he was out and the Beaumont brothers were in. Even though Big Dan didn't care about the ranch, Luke had a feeling he'd certainly care about the fact that his sons were taking over and going against his wishes.

But Luke and his brothers felt that their mother wouldn't have wanted to see the ranch go into disrepair. They'd fix it up in honor of her memory.

No matter how they sugar-coated what had just happened in the lobby of the courthouse, Luke dreaded his father's reaction.

As ASSIGNED BY Captain Fitz, Amber had to direct traffic safely out of the courthouse parking lot onto Main Street. She stood in the middle of the street, dividing the traffic into those turning right and those turning left to quickly clear out the parking lot. It was one of those boring jobs that the other deputies hated, and the Cap felt that was perfect for her.

But she wasn't going to feel down. She'd just done a fabulous deed in keeping the Beaumont Ranch in the hands of the Beaumonts and away from the hands of outside investors.

"Well, if it ain't my daughter the sergeant. What is our pillar of justice doing now?"

Her father, dressed in greasy coveralls, a greasy baseball cap and greasy sneakers, slapped the back of her crisp white uniform blouse with a hand.

"I'm directing traffic, Dad. Can't you see? Get to the curb. You can't be here in the middle of the traffic with me."

"I'll take full responsibility, Sergeant."

"Oh, for heaven's sake." She positioned her arms to direct drivers. "What brings you downtown?"

"I had to go to the license place."

That did her heart good. He was doing something according to the law.

"If I didn't get my license, you can bet you cops would be all over me."

"And I'd be leading the charge," Amber said, blowing her whistle at a particularly fast car. "Slow down! Tell me what you want, Dad. I'm a little busy here, and, again, I don't want you to get hurt in this traffic."

"I never get a chance to see you, daughter."

"Dad!" She blew her whistle at another car. "Spill it or get to the sidewalk and we'll talk later."

"I want you to move back home to the bosom of your family."

"The what?" She laughed. "You mean you want me to cook, clean and keep the law off your back."

He shrugged. "Guilty. Will you come home?"

"When pigs fly, Dad." She knew her father was teasing her, but she'd never leave her cute apartment over the Happy Tea Pot and China Shop unless she was moving out of town for a state police job. "Now get to the sidewalk, please."

"Come over for dinner and we'll discuss. Kyle is picking up some chicken and ribs and those corn muffins that you like from Smokin' Sammy's House of Hickory."

Yum. She did like Smokin' Sammy's.

"I'll come over for dinner. Thanks for the invitation." She smiled. He was so transparent. He knew it, and she knew it. "But I don't want any talk of me moving in. Wait a minute, you're not still moonshining, are you?"

He didn't answer, but she held up traffic while he walked to the sidewalk. He clutched at his heart. "Amber—I mean,

Sergeant Chapman, how can you ask me such a thing? I'm as pure as the newly fallen snow."

She laughed at his theatrics. Her father could always make her laugh.

"What about my brothers?"

"The same. They ain't making moonshine."

"They'd better not be!"

"Six o'clock?"

"I'll be there, Dad."

The traffic had dwindled to a few cars. It was then that she saw Luke Beaumont exit the courthouse and walk to the lot.

He waved to her and she walked toward him.

"What luck, huh?" he asked.

"Huh?"

"That you had to ask those three guys to leave because of the fire code."

"Oh. Yes."

"I found out that they were going to bid on the ranch. I'm not sure I could have outbid them. That was a close one."

"Good." Amber nodded. "I'm very happy for you."

He chuckled. "I didn't know that the Beaumont Sheriff's Department were sticklers for fire code violations."

"Oh. We are. Absolutely. It's very important to enforce all codes as that are on the books."

That sounded pompous, but she didn't want Luke to think that he was receiving special treatment from her because he was a Beaumont.

Nor did she want him to think she had helped him because she was some kind of devoted fan.

She did it for the town.

"I'm off duty, Luke. Do you need a ride?"

"Since I taxied right from the airport, I was going to hitchhike to visit my father in rehab, but I'm not ready to deal with him yet. Would you mind driving me out to the ranch? Hopefully my truck is there and working, and I can drive up and see my dad later, but, yeah, I'd appreciate a ride home. Thanks."

She radioed Dispatch that she was off duty and pointed to her cherry-red Honda CRV. "That's my car."

They walked to her car and Amber clicked open the locks. "Hop in."

Chapter Four

It was about fifteen miles to the ranch; most of it was highway except for the last five. They made small talk about the weather, bull riding and the town in general. Amber was careful not to talk about the condition of his ranch. Luke would see it soon enough.

"What happened to the entry arch?" he asked as they arrived.

"Hurricane Daphne. The storm is responsible for pretty much everything."

"Hmm…the entry arch is the first thing I'm going to fix."

It contained the logo of the Beaumont Ranch, five ornate B's in a circle for Big Dan, Valerie Lynn and their three boys. It was made of wrought iron, from what Amber remembered, and every vehicle and pedestrian passed under that arch.

Obviously, it bothered Luke that the symbol of his family was on the ground.

"Hang on." He got out of her car and pulled the arch to the side of the driveway.

He got back in and she started up the long drive to the homestead. Luke stuck his head out the window as they passed by several outbuildings in need of repair.

"Dammit!" he shouted. "Look at those wrecked buildings."

"I'm sorry, Luke."

The homestead came into sight. The roof had collapsed in the middle and the land that used to be around it was either bare or choked with weeds. Amber remembered beautiful flowers around the home—Valerie Lynn Beaumont had had a green thumb—but whatever had once bloomed had vanished. The portico had collapsed, twisted, and was hanging on by a couple of thick boards someone had propped up against the main portion.

"That has to be replaced," Luke said.

Two of the big picture windows had also blown out and were covered by sheets of plywood.

The whole place was in need of paint, but that was probably the least of his problems. He had yet to look inside. There was no need for a key. The door was half off its hinges.

"Let's go in, Amber. I might as well see inside."

"That's okay. I'll stay here."

"C'mon with me. Please."

She got the impression that he didn't want to be alone when he saw the condition of the homestead that had been in his family for generations.

"Okay," she finally said, feeling like she was intruding on something private. Something that was strictly reserved for the family that belonged there.

Too bad she didn't have the same feelings about the sad little bungalow in the middle of a junkyard. That was just a place where her parents fought about everything from rusted car parts to illegal moonshine.

When she looked around at the inside of the Beaumont ranch house, she wanted to cry.

Magnificent Stickley furniture had warped and was unsalvageable except as firewood. Fabulous blankets and baskets were covered in mud. Actually, the whole floor was warped and muddy. The beehive fireplace in the middle of the room had cracked and the remnants had fallen to the ground. Black mold crept up the walls.

It broke her heart to see family treasures destroyed. Some might be able to be saved, but most of what she'd seen would have to be trashed.

There were pictures and portraits of some long-ago Beaumonts. Some were intact, some had watermarks and were bulging out of their frames.

Amber turned to Luke, whose mood seemed to be alternating between sad and mad.

She wanted to hug him, but felt that was too forward. They'd only been high school acquaintances, nothing more. She hoped he didn't know that she'd had a crush on him since Mrs. Maloney's first grade.

So here she was at thirty years old without having a serious boyfriend at the present.

Most of the time, she was too focused on her career. She was devoted to keeping Beaumont a safe place for everyone to live, in which children would thrive.

To that end, she coached mixed teams of soccer, softball and basketball, and led the Beaumont children's chorus and drama club.

She divided her marriage "close calls" into three categories, although there were probably more. The cops were too full of themselves and moved on to their next conquests; the adventurers were too hyper and moved on; and the playboy types found younger women.

They all left her about when they figured out she was

more devoted to the job than to them. But they always parted as friends, having mutually enjoyed themselves.

It would only take four steps to walk in Luke's direction and wrap him in a comforting hug.

Sergeant Amber Chapman, who had arrested some of the worst criminals in the county, had to decide if she was woman enough to embrace Luke Beaumont or stay rooted where she was like a big blue chicken with a badge.

OH!

Luke took a step back in pure shock when he saw Amber's face and noticed her arms move. It seemed like she was about to cry and hug him at the same time.

No way. He had to be wrong. She didn't even like him. But maybe she was feeling sorry for him.

That was it!

But he didn't want any pity. Not from Amber Chapman; not from anyone.

The Beaumonts would pick themselves up by their bootstraps and put things right, even if they had to ride every rank bull from here to Australia and everywhere in between to get the money to rebuild.

The Beaumont Ranch would be restored to its former self.

"I'm not going to rest until there are cattle on the hill again, rank rough stock in the field and prize horses in the barns. And the ranch house will be just like my mother left it."

He didn't realize that he spoke the words out loud until Amber replied, "Good for you, Luke. Don't forget to hire the town people back. They've worked hard for the Beaumonts. You don't know the half of it."

He looked around and saw the boarded-up windows and remembered the propped-up portico. "I think I do."

Outside, he heard yelling and shouting and the tinny sound of cowbells ringing.

"What's that?" he asked, walking over to the front door.

Amber followed him. "I hear it, too."

On the way, Amber disturbed a pyramid of beer cans. Some thin, white rolling papers, which were sprinkled on the floor, attached themselves to her foot. Remnants of the kids' parties, she assumed.

Luke upset a drawer full of mice and they scattered like pool balls all over the room.

What a mess his home had become.

The noise outside became louder. It was several of the townspeople leading horses, bulls and cows and more toward the house.

"Welcome home, Luke!" shouted a man in a rumpled cowboy hat and a poncho, leading a gigantic bull.

"We're glad you won the auction. Hope you're staying and fixing the place up, Luke."

Luke recognized the neighbor from his position on the porch where the front door used to be. "I am, Santiago. I am. My brothers and I will be working hard this summer to restore the old place."

"Good!" Santiago grinned and cheers went up, loud enough to spook a couple of horses.

Amber arrived next to him, and he moved over so she could see. He slipped an arm around her waist to steady her.

"This is your stock that we are bringing back, Luke. We kept the animals for you—the ones that Mr. Beaumont gave to us. Big Dan—he just doesn't care," said Michelle Goldsmith, another neighbor.

"I know." Luke nodded.

"We've been taking care of them until someone returned. They are yours now," Santiago said.

Luke shook his head. "I can't thank you enough, but you all should keep them. You've been providing for them, so they should be yours."

"That's what friends are for," Michelle said. "We'll put some of the horses in the paddock and the rest in the pasture. All right? No arguing with us, Luke."

"I feel so…humbled," he whispered, and he doubted if anyone could hear him. Well, maybe Amber heard. He glanced at her and knew that she'd definitely heard. She was wiping away tears,

"What a beautiful thing to do," she said, her voice cracking.

Luke felt his own eyes stinging at such a caring gesture, even after Big Dan had left them without jobs.

He swallowed hard. "Thank you, my friends. For once, I am speechless."

"More will be returned when word gets out that you're back. By the way, nice riding in Billings," said Slim Gomez, the long-term foreman of the Beaumont Ranch.

Luke nodded. "When I'm done getting the house fixed up, we are going to have a barbecue the likes of which Beaumont has never seen."

Amber let out a little squeal. She must be a woman who liked her barbecue.

Then he noticed that Amber suddenly swayed and was about to fall on some stacked boards probably from the portico. Rusty nails peppered the boards.

Luke caught her. It was as if he was dipping her at the

end of a dance. Not that he ever did that, but it was good to know that he could do it!

He stared into her stunning green eyes. They were round with surprise.

"You were going to fall," he explained, barely breathing. She felt so good in his arms.

"I-I know. You can let me up now. Someone is giving us a wolf whistle outside."

"Sure."

He let her up and looked back at the parade of animals in front of him. "Need help?" he asked.

"Uh…no. You can go back to what you were doing." Florence, who owned nearby Star S, laughed.

Everyone joined in laughing.

"Is that Sergeant Chapman?" Florence asked.

Amber waved to her from a more secure position. "Yes, Flo. It's Amber."

"Good for you. Carry on." Florence gave her two thumbs-up.

Luke noticed that Amber's face was turning a bright pink.

"Don't mind them," Luke said.

She waved her hand, dismissing the idea. "Um, I'm not."

Luke pointed to another group walking up the driveway. "I'd better go help them, Amber. I'll be right back."

"Of course. Go ahead and get the animals situated."

He had so much to do, it got his blood pumping, just like when he rode bulls. He'd always loved ranch work and to be home for a while with a list of improvements and to be surrounded by friends—well, he was going to enjoy every minute.

And it felt so natural to hold Amber in his arms and

look deep into her green eyes. If he didn't know any better, by the way she studied his lips in anticipation, he'd think that she was interested in him.

But he knew better. Amber didn't have much use for him. In fact, she had to drag him back to Beaumont in order for him to take care of his legacy.

"I'd better buy some feed and hay," he said, thinking out loud.

Amber checked her watch. "You have to eat, too. How about dinner at the crazy Chapman household in a couple of hours? One of my brothers is picking up barbecue."

"I've been thinking of just that. Thanks. I'd love to." He jumped from the opening, as if he were a superhero, and was gone.

LOOKING AROUND, AMBER found a broom in the kitchen pantry and a box of garbage bags. Perfect. She might as well help out while Luke was tending to his stock.

The first thing she was going to do was to change from her uniform. She had workout gear in her car. That'd do.

Then she was going to get rid of the chickens and mice, right the furniture and sweep. The big, thick Mexican tiles needed to be washed several times, but they had to be swept first.

So, what was she doing helping Luke?

She had a feeling that he was overwhelmed. Bringing some of the stock back could have waited until tomorrow, but these were the animals that Big Dan hadn't sold. He'd just told his workers to help themselves. He probably hadn't counted on them being taken care of and brought back.

That's what friends are for.

Amber swept all the trash by the beer cans. Anything

with fur or feathers, she scooted out the back door the best she could.

A cat ran into the room and perched itself on top of the couch as if it had done the same thing many times before.

Cautiously, she approached the gray and black cat. It wore a collar and let her pet it, so it wasn't feral. Her tag showed that her name was Miss Kitty. "Okay, Miss Kitty, clear out the mice, please."

The cat sat there like a princess, cleaning her paws. "Let's go, Miss Kitty."

Nothing.

She abandoned the idea of any help from the cat and went back to sweeping.

All the water-stained pictures she put into a garbage bag with the intention of telling Luke that there was a fabulous restorer at the Beaumont Historical Society who could probably do wonders with them. She filled three garbage bags with pictures and loaded them into the back of her SUV.

Amber opened windows that were still intact and let the place air out.

She was just sweeping the dust, dirt and fallen chunks of plaster into the last garbage bag when Luke scared her by vaulting back into the room.

"Amber! Thanks so much, but you didn't have to do all that work." He looked around. "What a difference! There might be hope for the place yet."

"You can fix everything up, Luke. You and your brothers. And I'll help. So will my brothers. After all, I brought you back here. And as long as you can supply lumber, paint, nails and shingles, your friends and neighbors will help, too."

"Thanks. Thanks for everything. Now, let's go to your family's house and have barbecue. I'm starving."

"Help me shut the windows and we'll go," Amber said.

"Leave them open. I'll stay here tonight."

"You can't, Luke. Black mold. It's not healthy."

"Then I'll take a look at the bunkhouse. Maybe that fared better."

The bunkhouse wasn't much better. The floor was slimy and the mattresses were mildewed.

"Let's check out the barn. I could sleep in one of the stalls."

The barn was on higher ground, but all the ruined hay had to be removed. The cobwebs hung like Christmas tinsel, and the spiders were busy making their webs. There was a hole in the barn roof.

She shuddered thinking of all the spiders dropping on her like rain from the sky. "Let's get out of here, Luke."

The barn had to be readied for the horses as soon as humanly possible.

He shrugged, taking it all in stride. "I'll tent outside. I think our old camping supplies are here somewhere. You know us cowboys. Nothing like sleeping under the stars."

Amber almost snorted, but changed it in mid-snort to a fake cough. She'd bet her next paycheck that a bull riding star like Luke Beaumont hadn't slept in less than a three-star hotel in several years.

He opened a wooden cabinet and fished out a forest-green nylon bag—probably his tent—a couple of rolled-up sleeping bags and a lantern.

She was just about to invite him to stay at her apartment on the couch, but she couldn't form the words. It was just too soon.

Her face heated. That was a dumb thing to even think.

Why would she even think about inviting him to stay with her?

Maybe she was just too scared to get close to Luke. Her past record with men was like throwing nothing but gutter balls on the bowling alley of life.

"Isn't there any other place you can stay?" she asked.

"My father's in rehab, so I can't stay with him. He has an apartment in town, but it's a senior citizen place and they have rules. And I've pretty much lost touch with my gang from high school and college. It's hard to keep in touch with my friends when I'm never home."

"I imagine it would be."

He chuckled. "But once in a while, someone from home shows up in my autograph line."

She noticed that he didn't refer to her as a friend.

Amber didn't know why that tweaked her. So what if he didn't consider her one? She would rather consider herself a friend of the town of Beaumont.

Some friend she was. She couldn't wait to get out of Beaumont and get a job with the state police.

"You can't stay here," she blurted. "Go to the Beaumont House. It's been updated and it's quite a nice hotel now."

"I'd rather stick around here. Besides, I don't know if my old truck is working to go back and forth to get supplies and to visit Big Dan."

"Let's give your truck a try," she said. "I could always give it a jump."

But no matter what they did, the ancient, faded red Ford 150 truck wouldn't start.

She checked her watch. "Let's get going over to my father's house, Luke. You have to be hungry."

He slammed the hood shut. "I don't suppose you're getting the barbecue from—"

"Smokin' Sammy's House of Hickory?"

"Yeehaw! It's been a long time since I've had Smokin' Sammy's."

"One of my brothers is picking it up," Amber advised, pointing to her car. "There will be plenty, but let's get going. That is, unless you'd rather not go to the Chapman lair."

Luke stopped walking and pushed back his cowboy hat with his thumb. "Why would you say that?"

"Our families never got along. Let's face it. The Beaumonts are the town's leading citizens and the Chapmans lived on the other side of the tracks."

"We were busy ranching and your family was busy—"

"Moonshining," she said. "And selling hot car parts."

Amber continued to be embarrassed by her family. She hated the jokes that inevitably came her way and supposed she should have laughed along, but she didn't find them funny.

"I didn't say that."

"You didn't have to. Everyone knows. And everyone enjoyed our moonshine, including the—"

"Beaumonts." Luke grinned. "The Chapmans make the best moonshine."

"*Made* the best moonshine. Past tense. My father and brothers are out of the business."

Amber opened the door of her red Honda and Luke went around the front to the passenger side. "I really appreciate you driving me around."

Amber started her car. "After dinner, if you'd like, I'll take you to see your father."

"No. You've done enough. I'll hitchhike over."

"Hitchhiking is illegal in Beaumont County," she said in her best cop voice.

"It's really not a problem. You could always rent a car at Willie Greenfield's when he opens in the morning until you get your wheels working."

"Sounds like a plan. Good idea."

She laughed. "I got a million good ideas for you."

Chapter Five

Luke had to look twice to locate the Chapman place.

It had gotten much worse since the last time he'd been home.

The sad-looking ranch house sat in the middle of a junkyard just inside the Beaumont town limits. In fact, when people read the Welcome to Beaumont sign, the first thing on their left was the Chapman place.

It looked like it needed a couple coats of paint, which should be easy judging by the rows of rusted paint cans dotting a little patch of lawn. Junk cars and shelving units stuffed with car parts dwarfed the house.

Ninety-nine point nine percent of the town looked on this junkyard as a blight on the historic, nice-looking town. It was common knowledge that several townspeople kept an eye on the tax rolls, hoping that Marv Chapman would slip up and not pay his taxes. Then they could buy the house at auction and level everything.

Funny, now the Beaumont Ranch, which spread its acres behind the town like a benevolent kingdom, was a blight in its present condition, too.

Thinking of the two families made him feel miserable. How ironic it was that his father was an alcoholic and Amber's father made booze. Maybe he should have befriended Amber earlier, in high school, but it had never crossed his mind, a mind full of riding bulls and gold belt buckles.

Neither of them was like their father, and they both had to bear the emotional scars.

"You know, Luke. I was just thinking… My brothers are pretty good with a hammer. Maybe they can help you rebuild."

It was just on Luke's lips that charity begins at home, but he had no right to say such a thing. Then it dawned on him that it would bring him closer to Amber, and he liked that idea. Then again, he hated to ask for help.

"Thanks. But I don't want to bother them. They probably have better things to do."

"That's what we do here in Beaumont," she said. "We help our neighbors."

"I can pay as long as our money lasts and my brothers keep winning."

She turned off her car. "That's not what I meant."

"I know, but I think that a guy should be paid for his labor."

"And I think that neighbors should help neighbors. You can provide the food and drink."

He nodded as he waited for Amber to lead the way up the rotted stairs to the front door of her father's house.

She pointed. "Watch this rotted lumber." She stepped over the offensive boards.

"Got it."

On the front porch, she knocked on the door then walked in. "I brought us some company."

"Why, Luke Beaumont." Marv Chapman pulled him into what Luke assumed was the family room. "Welcome."

He shook his hand. "Thanks, Mr. Chapman."

Amber gave her father a hug. "I brought Luke with me. He just got the ranch back at auction, and he's going to be hanging around town for a while fixing it up."

"Great to see you, Luke. Sorry about your ranch," Marv said. "Me and the boys hung up some plywood on your windows. Hope it did some good."

"I have you to thank?" he asked. "I really appreciate it."

"You have Amber to thank. She nagged us until we did it."

He looked over at Amber. She was shifting on her feet and looking uncomfortable.

He had her to thank for a lot of things. If she hadn't come to the autographing, the developers from Texas would be the new owners of the Beaumont Ranch.

There was so much more to her than the girl he once knew, and he'd like to get to know her better. He already knew that she had principles and loved Beaumont, and followed bull riding. They had that in common.

"Sit down, Luke. Sit down." Amber pointed to a chair.

He had to step around a motor hanging from a rack. After he sat, he saw hundreds of wooden crates containing canning jars in various sizes.

Amber must have noticed his surprise. "They're not moonshining anymore," Amber said again, apparently feeling the need to explain. "So, then, Dad, what the hell are all those jars doing here?"

"Storage. I'm simply storing them for now."

"I swear, Dad. If you are moonshining, I will—"

"Amber, stop. Will you quit being a cop for a while and just enjoy the evening with your family and Luke?"

"I can't. I know my family and what they're capable of. That's why Mom isn't here. Don't you get that?"

Marv Chapman swore under his breath and disappeared into the kitchen.

"Sorry, Luke. It's just our usual disagreement that we have to go through. I accuse and Dad denies. I didn't mean to make you uncomfortable."

"I'm fine. Matter of fact, when we visit my father later, I'll bet that our disagreement will make yours seem like a little speed bump."

Her father returned with a six-pack of beer. "I also have soda," Marv said. "But the beer is nice and cold. Luke?"

"A beer sounds good to me."

Luke popped the top and just about drained the can. It was cold and refreshing, and he didn't realize how thirsty he was.

There was a commotion on the porch and Amber's three brothers came crashing in. Luke remembered the ribbing they'd given him in high school. They'd continually called him the "Prince of Beaumont" and "Your Majesty." There was more, but he didn't want to go there. He remembered Amber telling them to be quiet, and she tried to move them along, but they'd pulled out of her grasp and shushed her as if she were a bothersome fly.

Maybe the Chapman Clowns—what he'd immaturely used to call them—had grown up.

The Chapman brothers each carried takeout bags. "Well, if it isn't Luke, Prince of Beaumont," said Ronnie.

Some things never change.

Mr. Chapman gestured with his hand. "You know my boys, Aaron, Ronnie and Kyle?"

Luke nodded. "Sure I do."

There were handshakes all around—strong, manly, hand-pumping handshakes.

Luke couldn't figure out if it was a show of strength or if they were actually glad to see him.

He'd never hung around with the Chapman brothers in school, all three were younger than he was, but he knew their reputation throughout the years. He remembered that Big Dan had hired them to work as barn hands, stating that they needed legitimate jobs. But when they'd learned they could make more money selling hooch than shoveling manure, they'd quickly quit.

"How ya doing, Your Majesty?" Kyle asked.

Aaron was not to be outdone. "We are your three humble subjects, Majesty."

Ugh!

"How've you all been?" he asked. "It's been a while."

"You're the one who has been shaking up the PBR. You're riding hot." Ronnie pumped his fist.

Kyle nodded. "My money's riding on you to win the PBR World Finals in Vegas."

"Well, then, for your sake, I'd better win." He made eye contact with Amber. "Besides, I need some money to fix up the ranch."

"You sure do, cowboy," Amber said.

Amber was setting the table and when that was done, she helped her brothers unpack the bags of food. The scent of hickory wafted around the kitchen and made Luke's mouth water.

"Let our guests help themselves first," Marv Chapman said. "So, you big galoots, that means Luke and Amber."

Ronnie laughed. "Amber's not a guest, she's my sister." He stabbed a pork rib with a fork and was just about to put it on his plate when Amber snatched it off.

"Nice one, sis!" Kyle said.

"Nice one, Amber," Luke echoed. "Quick reflexes. You'd make a good bull rider."

"No thanks. I have enough excitement being a cop."

"And I'll bet you're a good one," Luke said.

Amber turned to her father. "If I were a good cop, I'd find out how you guys are making a living. You all swear that you're not moonshining and that the junk business isn't what it used to be, so how are you earning a living, or shouldn't I ask?"

Luke noticed that neither her brothers nor her father would make eye contact with Amber. They had to be up to something. He'd bet his last dollar they were still moonshining. Or maybe he was being too judgmental and just assumed that they'd never stopped, and Amber was falling for their lies, but maybe he wasn't giving her enough credit. She was one sharp woman.

"Okay, let's change the subject," Amber's father said. "Luke, what are your plans in rehabbing the ranch? It needs a lot of *rehab*."

"Yeah. A lot of *rehab*," said Ronnie.

Kyle laughed. "Rehab the ranch and rehab Big Dan."

"Knock it off!" Amber looked up at Luke from her place across the table. "I apologize for my family's lack of manners."

He shrugged. Luke made a split decision not to let any of the Chapmans get to him with their kidding—and they were notorious for kidding. Although sometimes it had bothered him, now wasn't one of those times.

Maybe it was because Amber was sitting across the table looking at him with concerned green eyes. Besides, she'd already stuck up for him a couple of times.

Or maybe it was simply the Smokin' Sammy's that

put him in a good mood, and Amber's defense of him put him in an even better mood.

"In answer to your question, the place needs a lot of fixing. And since you gentlemen—" he looked pointedly at Amber's three brothers "—apparently have nothing to do, I could use your help. It'll be a paid gig for as long as our money holds out—my brothers' and mine."

"We're kinda busy, Luke," Aaron said.

"Okay. My mistake."

"It's my mistake, too, brothers dearest," Amber said sarcastically. "For I can't imagine what on earth you could be doing, legally that is."

"It all comes back to that, doesn't it, little sis?" Ronnie asked.

Kyle shrugged. "Are the Chapman brothers on the right or the wrong side of the law?"

"Knock it off. You three are giving me indigestion," Marv said. "You all know I promised Amber that we are going strictly legit until further notice. Maybe forever."

"Forever?" Kyle asked, pretending to clutch his heart.

"What do we live on?" asked Ronnie.

"And that brings us full circle," Amber said. "You know, maybe you could clean out this pigsty. It's a cross between a car repair shop and a bottle return."

"But for once, I'll bet our house is better looking than Luke's," her father said.

"The county landfill looks better than the Beaumont homestead," Luke said, helping himself to more ribs. "It's going to take a lot of hard work, but I'm up for it."

"That's the spirit, Luke," Marv said. "And the three of us are going help you. Starting tomorrow. Our business can wait."

"Make it the four of us," Amber said. "I have the day off."

"I'll put the word out. We'll get some neighbors, too," Marv said.

"Thanks. I appreciate it," Luke said. "I'll get supplies first thing in the morning."

"Go tonight. The lumberyard is open until nine o'clock. It's only seven now," said Marv.

"I wanted to see my father tonight. Remember? He's the one in *rehab*?"

"Whenever you're ready, I'll drive you," Amber said. "The boys can clean up."

Funny how he'd rather stay and talk to the Chapmans than have to tell his father that he was no longer the owner of the Beaumont Ranch.

"I'm ready now," Luke said.

Amber stood, as did Luke. He shook hands. "See you tomorrow, then. Thanks for the grub. I was dreaming of Smokin' Sammy's."

"Oh, and, Ronnie, how about fixing Luke's truck? We did all we could. Your expertise is needed."

Ronnie blew on his nails and buffed them on his shirt. "My expertise, sis?"

"Don't let it go to your head," she joked.

Amber opened the door and Luke held it for her to pass through.

They walked onto the porch. "Let's get this over with," Luke mumbled. "I'm dreading it, but I'd like the company." And he did want her company. There was something about Amber that calmed him and had him confiding in her.

"I'll wait in the lobby of the place until you're done

visiting. I'm probably the last person on earth that Big Dan wants to see."

Luke chuckled. "Not after he hears what I have to say."

Chapter Six

The Beaumont County Alcohol and Drug Rehabilitation Facility was a sprawling brick-and-wood building that sat on a hill on the northern corner of town. It was surrounded by rolling fields of green grass, and everyone joked that it would make a good clubhouse and golf course.

It was ironic to Luke that the rehab facility was on land donated by his grandfather, whose namesake was residing there.

Grandpa Beaumont would be ticked.

At least he wasn't sitting in the opposite corner of the town in the Beaumont County Correctional Facility.

Although that was still a possibility if Big Dan didn't do what he should.

They approached the reception desk on the right of the lobby.

"I'm here to see—" Luke began.

"Mr. Daniel Beaumont," said the cute receptionist with rosy red cheeks and the same hair color.

"And I'm—"

"Luke Beaumont, his son, and bull riding star." She giggled. "Can I have your autograph?" She held out a black felt-tip pen and rolled up her sleeve.

Amber rolled her eyes. "Patricia O'Prell, don't you have paper, for heaven's sake? It's an autograph, not a tattoo."

"Yes, Sergeant Chapman," said Patty in a singsong voice as she pulled out some paper.

Luke spoke as he wrote. "To Patty—is that with a 'y'?" Just as he asked, he saw her nameplate. "To Patty with a Y. Thanks for being a fan of the PBR. Best wishes, Luke Beaumont."

"Thanks, Luke! Are you going to win the Finals in Vegas?"

"You betcha! Now, Patty, how do I find my father?"

She clicked her computer keys and pointed. "Down that hall in the community room. Sign the visitor's book, Luke. You, too, Sergeant."

"I'm just going to hang around the lobby," Amber said.

"Please come with me." Luke took her hand and she looked shocked. He dropped it. Maybe she just wasn't ready for handholding, but he sure as hell wanted her touch. And it shocked him how much he was relying on Amber. "I would like you to come. You have nothing to hide. You were doing your job, and Big Dan would have probably been in prison if you hadn't intervened."

"Okay. But he's only one of many that I placed in here. I don't think that any of them want to see me."

Luke chuckled. "Don't worry. I'll protect you."

"Sign the visitor's book, Sergeant Chapman," Patty said again as she held out a pen, and Amber signed.

"Nice." She tacked Luke's autograph to the bulletin board on the wall behind her. "Good luck, Luke." She stood and blew him a kiss.

Amber's eyes grew round. "Patricia O'Prell!"

"Well, he's not married yet. Besides, everyone's a fan of the Beaumont Big Guns, and Luke is the best of the Beaumonts."

Amber swallowed hard. "Yes. He's a good bull rider."

Luke continued to walk but turned his head and said, "Only good?"

"Oh, for heaven's sake!" Amber sputtered.

"You're totally wonderful, Luke!" Patty yelled.

This time Amber turned back and raised her eyebrows. She wanted this young woman to quit flirting with her... with her...

Darn. She wasn't exactly sure what exactly Luke was to her. An old schoolmate? A crush that she couldn't shake?

Patty tossed her hair. "I'm so sorry, Sergeant Chapman. I didn't know that you and Luke are dating, that you're a couple."

Amber swallowed. "We are *not* a couple."

"Oh, then you're just dating—"

Sergeant Chapman took Luke's hand and led him down the hallway. "I know where to find Big Dan. I've been here a million times."

"Oh, I thought you were just pulling me toward a dark, quiet corner."

Amber's face heated. If he only knew how many times she'd dreamed of being with Luke Beaumont in a dark, quiet corner and what they would do together.

But now was not the time.

He'd be touring again soon, and she expected to be transferred out of town when she joined the state police. They didn't have a future together. They never had one.

But she could dream.

Amber reminded herself that she'd brought Luke back

to Beaumont to get him to fix up his ranch and put some unemployed citizens who were in dire straits back to work.

She hadn't brought him back to date her.

What about a fling?

No way. She wasn't the type to fling and flee. Just sex seemed so impersonal. When she fell for someone, it meant so much more. It also hurt a lot more when a breakup was inevitable.

If she was the fling and flee type, she'd have a fling with Luke Beaumont and once and for all get him out of her system.

Luke's cell phone rang.

He had to drop Amber's hand. He didn't want to, because it felt good, and for once she didn't pull away. Maybe he was making progress in getting Amber's attention.

"Sorry. I have to take this call. It's my brother, Jesse. I hope nothing's wrong."

He checked his watch, but it didn't do him any good. He never could remember how many hours, if any, Tucson was behind Oklahoma.

He slid the screen and hit the green button. "What's up, Jesse?"

Amber was walking, and Luke fell into place beside her.

"Hey, Luke," Jesse said. "Reed won the afternoon event. He even rode the bounty bull, Big Bad Leroy, for ninety-two points. Reed's still negotiating the payout."

"What do you mean?" Luke asked. As far as he always knew, the bounty grew in five-thousand-dollar increments whenever the bounty bull wasn't ridden. When someone finally rode that bull, it was winner-takes-all. "What's the total payout?"

"Thirty-five thousand."

Luke whistled. "Did he win the round, too?"

"You know it!"

"But…" Jesse paused. "Reed's negotiating the payout in cattle instead of cash from a couple of the stock contractors here." Jesse chuckled. "Plus, he's going to have them shipped to our ranch and wants some breeding stock."

"Reed could talk the ears off an elephant," Luke said. "I'd give him whatever he wanted just to shut him up."

"After a couple more cold ones, it looks like that's just what those boys are going to do—give Reed what he wants."

Luke smiled. "So there are going to be cattle grazing again at the Beaumont Ranch."

He liked how Amber's eyes lit up after he said this. She was just about as happy as he was, and that did his soul good.

It puzzled him as to how much he cared about making her happy. Before she showed up at the autographing at the Oklahoma City arena, he hadn't thought about Amber that much.

But he hadn't forgotten her, like he had some of his other classmates. He'd always remember her crying as she'd walked home from the prom. Undoubtedly, Amber blamed him for what had happened, and he didn't have the heart to tell her that her date, Crazy Kenny Fowler, was the one who had spread the story that he'd been bribed with Chapman moonshine to take her to the prom, and then had gotten insulting and vulgar about Amber.

That just wasn't the cowboy way. Not that Kenny cared.

But Luke cared back then. Maybe he still did.

He said his goodbyes to Jesse and told him to call back when he had more details. "One more thing, Jess." Luke sighed. "I am just about to visit Dad here at the rehab place. I am going to update him as to the Beaumont property. You think I should tell him about the stock?"

"That's up to you, big brother. He's going to find out eventually, if he hasn't already. Small town."

"Yeah." Luke hated to shake up his father, especially when he was in rehab. He didn't want to give him any excuse to start drinking again, but that was a hopeless goal. "Later, bro."

"Sorry, Amber, but that was my brother, Jesse. He said that Reed scored big money at the Tucson bull riding, and he's taking stock in trade."

Amber gave him a thumbs-up. "So, there will be cattle dotting the hills again?"

"There will be!"

AMBER COULD TELL just when Luke realized where they were and what they were doing. It was like all the air left the place and went somewhere else.

The twinkle left Luke's eyes and his smile was forced.

"Here we are in the residents' housing. Room 4009. Are you okay?" Amber asked him when the color left his face.

"I'm okay. I just have to switch gears now and visit the old man. I hate the thought of catching him up to date. This isn't going to be pretty. Maybe you shouldn't go in with me and wait in the lobby like you suggested."

Amber smiled widely and knocked on the door.

"Come in! Come in! About time I got some visitors." Big Dan Beaumont's voice invaded every nook and corner of the rehab facility.

The door swung open, and Amber shifted on her feet. "I was just about to go to the lobby and wait, Mr. Beaumont, so you can visit with Luke in private."

She looked at Luke and noticed the shock on his face. Like she'd told him before, Big Dan was a shadow of his former self. His gray hair stuck out in every direction, and he was hunched over as if he didn't have any bones in his body. That's what drinking and not caring about anything or anyone could do to someone.

No. That wasn't true. According to Big Dan's probation officer, he desperately loved and missed his deceased wife, Valerie Lynn, who died two years ago, and he didn't want to live without her.

"Get in here, Sergeant. You know more about me than I do," Dan shouted. "Come in!"

Luke turned to Amber. "C'mon, Amber. My father has spoken."

"And they heard him over in Plainville, too," Amber whispered.

Luke chuckled. "Let's go into your room, Dad."

"This isn't my room. I live on Main Street in an apartment building that someone else owns and is full of us old folks," he snapped.

"Then let's go into *that* room," Luke pointed. "The one that has your name on the nameplate."

"Okay."

They all took a chair by a small round table in front of a window. There was also a small fridge and a microwave in the room, a hospital-type bed, a dresser and a TV on a corner cabinet.

"This is a far cry from how the ranch used to be, Dad. How long do you have to stay in here?"

"Until I'm cured, I guess," he said. "Wait. I'm wrong. I'll never be cured. I'll always be an alcoholic—at least that's what they tell me."

"You're hearing what they're saying, Mr. Beaumont? That's fabulous. Do you believe it?" Amber asked.

"Call me Big Dan." He sniffed. "And I'm not powerless over alcohol. I can quit anytime I want. I just don't want to."

"Then, Dad, you're going to stay in here for a long time." Luke let out a deep breath. "And I have something to tell you, but I don't want you to have any setbacks."

"You mean that you bought the ranch out from under me?"

"I didn't. I mean that—" Luke's eyes grew wide. "How did you know?"

"Small town," he and Amber said in unison. They all laughed, and that cleared the air.

"Dad, all of us boys chipped in and bought the ranch. It's still yours, but there's just some auction rule that it has to go in the bidder's name. That was me. I was the bidder because Reed and Jesse are riding another circuit while the PBR is on break. I took the break off."

"You should have stayed riding. You know my wishes. I wanted the ranch to stay as it was."

"Yeah. You wanted the place to go to ruin while you're drinking and fighting and making a damn fool out of yourself. You're getting arrested now, Dad."

Amber stayed silent. She really wished she had insisted and waited in the lobby. This was a family affair. Too bad that Luke's truck hadn't started. He wouldn't have needed her for rides. Then again, she liked being with him, liked his company.

Maybe her brother wouldn't be able to fix the truck, and she could continue giving Luke rides. Too bad Ronnie could fix anything. Her other brothers had nicknamed him "Wrench Hands."

Big Dan pounded a fist on the table, and it made Amber jump. "I wanted the ranch to stay the same as it was when Valerie Lynn died."

"But it's way beyond that. It's a big mess from Hurricane Daphne. And you know that Mom loved the history of that ranch. The old pictures, all the historic maps that were on the walls—gone! Water damage. The art that was priceless. Gone! The chair that Mom liked to sit in and crochet, mice were living in it and in the drawers. Kids have been partying in there."

Big Dan had a pained look on his face.

"But above all, the entrance sign with the five B's on it? That's down, Dad. And that represented our home. It represented the best upbringing a kid could have—all us kids. We want it back. I mean, I know we can't go back, but maybe our kids could experience what we had."

That last sentence surprised Dan, but it shocked Luke.

Luke stood and looked out the window. "Your neighbors brought some stock back today. They took care of things when you didn't. And Reed just called. He won on a bounty bull and was negotiating for stock to buy. The ranch is going to be restored with or without your approval, and I'm going to reemploy our workers that you didn't care about."

Another pound on the table. "I don't approve."

"It's out of your hands, Dad. Reed, Jesse and I own it

now," Luke said softly, evenly. "And it'll be our money that'll fix it up."

"Get out of here, Luke. I'm tired. Goodbye, Sergeant Chapman."

They both stood to leave. Amber offered her hand to shake his and Dan stood and took it. His hand was limp and clammy.

Luke offered his hand, too. Dan turned away. Luke let his hand drop at his side. "Okay. Let's get going, Amber. I think I've said all I've come to say."

Big Dan whirled around and put his hands on his hips. "I've got one more thing to say."

Luke looked like he had just gone eight seconds with an eighteen-hundred-pound Brahma bull. "Say it, Dad."

"Are you two in cahoots together? I mean, Sergeant Chapman arrests me and puts me in here so I can't get out and stop you, and you go and buy the place out from under me, and I can't get out and stop you."

Now, that was offensive! Amber was just about to say something when Luke took her hand.

"Cahoots? Amber and I are friends, yes. And do we both want what's best for the ranch and for the town? Yes. But are we in cahoots? No."

"We'll see," said Big Dan.

Amber's heart was racing. She'd been accused of many things, but not trying to take a man's ranch from him with his son.

"There's nothing to see, Mr. Beaumont," Amber said. "There's nothing—"

"Forget it, Amber," Luke said. "Let's head out. It's been a long day and I have to make up my camp outside since the ranch is full of black mold."

"There're hotels in town," his father snapped.

"I'd rather be home, Dad. After such a long time on the road, there's nothing like being home, but you wouldn't get that."

Dan leaned toward them. "I can get that. I'm not stupid."

"Well, then, for heaven's sake, that's why I want to be home, Dad. I'm sick of hotels, and I like camping, you know that. Besides, kids are partying in the house. I'll get rid of them." Luke took his hat off and raked his fingers through his hair. He was clearly frustrated.

Amber didn't know why his father was questioning Luke about pitching a tent on the property, but judging by the slight nudge he gave her, he wanted to leave. "Amber, are you ready to go?"

She faintly heard her name, but she was already in the hall and headed for the lobby to get the hell out of the place. Big Dan could be a pain in the butt to deal with when he was drunk, but he was in rare form when he was sober.

Amber had an empty feeling in her heart for Luke. She vowed to work herself to the bone to help the town...or was it Luke she wanted to help?

Chapter Seven

It was really pouring when they left the rehab center, and Amber ran to her car to avoid the majority of it. As she unlocked the doors, she realized that Luke wasn't with her.

In between her wipers clearing the windows, she saw Luke looking up at the sky and grinning as if he was taking a shower. He had taken his hat off and turned in a quick circle. Amber half expected him to start dancing.

Whatever he was doing, he certainly wasn't in a hurry to get out of the rain.

Finally he opened the passenger door and slid inside on the leather seats, which luckily were rainproof, mostly.

"Glad you have leather seats," he said.

"Just what I was thinking."

"I needed that!" He wiped his face with a shirtsleeve.

It must be something to do with washing away the stress after meeting with his father, Amber thought. Or maybe he just liked rain.

"Luke, you can't pitch a tent in this."

"You're probably right. I guess I should go to a hotel tonight. Would you mind dropping me somewhere?"

"I don't mind in the least. How about the Beaumont Inn or the Beaumont House?"

"Doesn't matter to me. Whichever one is the closest to the ranch."

They didn't say much of anything on the way to the inn. Since Luke had had a tough time with his father, he was probably processing it all.

When she got to the Beaumont Inn, it was raining harder than before. At least they had a portico.

Just as soon as Luke went in, he came out. "No room in the inn. The manager called over to the Beaumont House for me, and they are full, too."

"Wonder what's going on?"

"Freshman orientation and a band competition at the university. The manager said there isn't a room in the tri-county area."

"Ouch."

"Back to the tent idea," Luke said.

"You can't, Luke. You'd be swimming."

"I'd offer you my father's house, but you'd probably have to sleep on car parts. Or under the motor that's hanging in the dining room." She swore under her breath. "Maybe they are going to make a coffee table out of it. And here I thought if they'd clean the place up, my mother might come home to stay. But that's just wishful thinking."

"Did they ever divorce?" Luke asked.

"No. She still loves him. She keeps hoping that he'll change." She paused. "It would be nice if one of my brothers would move out and get his own place, but they're tied to Dad's coveralls."

Luke turned his hat around in a circle. "I don't have any close friends that I can mooch off of. I didn't really keep in touch. My loss."

"You didn't even keep in touch with Kenny Fowler?" she teased.

"No way in hell, but I did hear he'd moved to one of the Carolinas."

"The Southern one, but that isn't far enough away from me."

"I hear you."

"Listen, Luke. You're going to have to stay with me." A shot of electricity went through her, and she felt like a giddy teenager doing something sneaky for which she was going to be caught.

"You don't need me underfoot," he said. "I'll sleep in my pickup."

Amber laughed. "A bull riding star sleeping in his truck? It's not even a rock-star bus. Let's face it, if anyone found out that's what the town of Beaumont was doing to a local treasure, we'd be drummed out of Oklahoma."

"Treasure? After what we paid to bail out the ranch, I couldn't even buy you a drink."

She realized that she still had her uniform on. No drinking for her. Alcohol wasn't her drug of choice, anyway— pizza was—and then Smokin' Sammy's and the fried chicken place out on the Old Post Road, in that exact order.

Amber shook her head. She had to get fit or the state police wouldn't take her. And what happened to Marco's Fit-nasium? She kept thinking that she'd join, but never did.

"So, are you going to accept my invitation, Luke? As I see it, you don't have a choice and neither do I. Stay as long as you'd like. After working all day on your ranch, you're going to need a shower and a place to sleep. I have a comfortable couch."

"Thanks. For now, it makes sense. I accept your invitation, and will be out of your hair as soon as I fix up a bedroom and a bathroom at the ranch."

That was that. She'd just invited Luke to stay at her place and he'd accepted. When word got out that she was living with Luke, the gossip would rain like...rain!

As far as the town knew, she'd never dated much. None of the men she'd ever met could hold a candle to her long-term crush, Luke Beaumont.

Darn him!

Luke had put the town of Beaumont on the map. Now all he had to do was to put the Beaumont Ranch back on the tourist trail with the other historical landmarks and the town would thrive again.

If she had to give Luke Beaumont a place to stay, it would mean nothing to her. She'd be leaving Beaumont, and so would he.

"I live over the Happy Tea Pot and China Shop," she said. "It's a fairly new tearoom and store in the middle of Main Street. It sounds pretty girly, doesn't it?"

He chuckled. "Am I going to feel like a bull in a china shop?"

Amber laughed. "Not really. Out back, behind the shop, there's a separate door and staircase that goes to my apartment. You never have to feel like a bull in a china shop—that is, unless it reminds you of your job."

Out of the corner of her eye, she could see him lean over and stare at her. "A lot of people wouldn't agree with you. They think that bull riding isn't a job, that it's a hobby."

"You work hard. You jog, lift weights, you ride practice bulls and you even do yoga, so—"

"How do you know I do yoga?"

For heaven's sake, she sounded like a buckle bunny.

"Um, well… I saw you around town in high school, but you had to continue to train to get where you are. I think that the commentators on TV mentioned the yoga."

Luke touched her arm and she almost jumped through the roof of her car. She didn't expect the contact, but she liked it.

"Thanks for realizing how hard I work. Sometimes I wonder why I do it and don't work the ranch full-time."

"Do you love riding?"

"I do, but it doesn't leave me time to develop relationships with all the traveling I do, and one-night stands are not for me."

"I guess you have to take the good with the bad, and hope for more good. A lot of people don't like their jobs," Amber said.

"What about you? Do you like your job?"

"Sometimes. Most of the time. I wish I wasn't the only woman in a small department because I get what I call the 'girly' assignments—the things the captain doesn't want to give the guys. You see, he saves them for the real cop work. That's what I think, anyway."

"What do you mean?" Luke asked.

Amber took a deep breath and dumped what she'd been stewing over some eight years.

"I get a lot of traffic duty, like today. On one occasion, I stayed here and covered while the whole department, all five of them, went on a road trip to pick up a parole absconder in Comanche County. I could have done that alone. The man was short of ninety years old and was in a wheelchair! I get the petit larcenies. They get the robberies. Oh, and one of my perpetual duties is to enter or look up information on our computer systems, because they whine and claim that they are too old to learn computer skills and it takes me half the time, so I got the assignment. That kind of thing."

"That stinks."

"I've volunteered to train them yet again, watch as they work the various systems, but instead they just want me to do it *for* them. I've given up complaining, except now I've switched to whining."

"You're not whining. I asked you about it."

She felt like a chip fell off one of her shoulders and crumbled into dirt.

"Thanks for listening." She hit the defogger on her dash to clear the steam from her windshield. "A lot of hot air in here!"

"I saw you with the state police study guide. Is that what you really want? The state police?"

"I hope so. I need to move to a bigger department where I'm not the only woman."

Sheesh. Was it possible that the tax auction was just this morning when Luke had caught her reading the study guide? What a long day. The man must be exhausted.

"There's the Happy Tea Pot now," Amber said. "Every time I see that big, flowered teapot sporting a big smile on the sign, I smile, too. It cheers me up when I'm down."

"Are you down a lot?"

Amber made a left turn to park behind the Happy Tea Pot. "Not really. Only when my family gets to me— mostly my brothers. Well, my father, too. I don't trust them to stay out of trouble, because they seem to get a rush living on the fringe of criminal behavior."

"Your brothers have always lived on the fringe. Maybe they should try riding bulls. They can get their adrenaline rush legally."

"No, thanks. I want them legal, not dead," she said.

"Um, not that I want you dead, Luke. Oh, darn. You know what I mean."

It was time to change the subject.

She laughed. "Ready to make a run for it in the rain? Oh, wait. You love the rain."

"I do. It makes things grow, and it makes me feel alive. Don't you agree?"

"It just makes me feel wet." She grinned. "If I want to feel alive, I'll take a bath or a shower in the bathroom with scented soap."

Luke shook his head. "You don't know what you're missing."

Amber pointed. "There's the door. When you're done singing in the rain, come upstairs. I'll greet you with a fluffy towel, the kind you find in a bathroom."

Then it dawned on her. "Hey, do you have any clothes? I don't remember seeing—"

"My gear bag is on the floor of the back seat. So, don't worry. I won't be naked."

Her face was about to combust. "I didn't mean that. I meant that I could find you some sweats or something. You don't have to wear a towel, though you could if you'd like. Or you could walk around naked, if that's what you bull riders do."

She hoped that he thought she was flirting instead of feeling…nervous. It had been so long since she'd been this infatuated with a man—and that man was Luke. Now her infatuation was living and breathing and going to stay with her for a while. She had to calm down. She was acting like a rookie at love when actually she'd had a couple of relationships.

But she'd had no relationship with Luke, yet he was the one she'd always wanted. Maybe by spending time with him, she would finally get him out of her system. Maybe Luke would buck himself off that pedestal she had him on. Then she could move on and find a guy she could settle down with.

THIS HAS BEEN *a wild day*, Luke thought as he walked up the stairs to Amber's apartment. If anyone had ever told him that he'd be the official owner of the Beaumont Ranch, that the property would be in such a mess, that he'd eat barbecue among the car parts and canning jars at the Chapmans', that he'd visit his father in rehab and that he'd be staying with Amber Chapman, he would have laughed.

Yeah. What a day! And there was more to go. He knocked on the door of Amber's apartment and stood there, waiting, with his gear bag in hand, not quite believing that he was imposing on her like this.

He could have easily pitched a tent in the rain or even slept in his pickup. He could have cleared a spot in the barn with some version of clean hay, but the roof leaked so much, he'd be better outside.

In his early days of bull riding and driving from event to event, he and his traveling buddies slept wherever they landed, which was mostly in the car.

Amber opened the door and, as promised, she met him with a big towel.

"Thanks."

He took it and dried his hair. He should probably take his wet clothes off and put on something dry.

"Come in. I'll show you around," Amber said.

Her place was warm and inviting, and her couch with the stripes and matching pillows looked just as inviting. Suddenly he felt dead on his feet.

"The bathroom is down the hall on the right. You might want to shower or change or whatever."

"That sounds great, Amber."

"You'll see shampoo and liquid soap. If you can't find something you need, just yell. My house is your house. Don't ask, just help yourself."

He looked at her sparkling grass-green eyes and smiled. Amber was hot, and he couldn't wait to see her out of that uniform...and...uh—

Amber Chapman? What was he thinking?

He liked her loyalty to Beaumont, and liked her loyalty to her crazy family. He liked how she cared enough for his father to give him several chances and to get him into rehab. He liked how she was willing to roll up her sleeves and help him fix up the ranch.

Amber Chapman was quite a woman, but he'd never thought of her as hot...until now.

"I think I'll take you up on that shower."

"Be my guest. Would you like something to eat? I can make you a ham-and-cheese sandwich on rye. Or if you want something sweet, I have chocolate-chip cookies."

"Did you make them?"

"I did, and they are divine."

"Homemade chocolate-chip cookies are my downfall," Luke said, already drooling.

"Then get ready to fall down."

His cell phone rang. "It's Reed. I have to take this."

Amber nodded and disappeared into the back of the apartment. Her bedroom, maybe.

"Hey, Reed. What's up?"

"Bro, there're ten truckloads of cattle, a handful of bulls, and a lot of rodeo stock headed your way from Charlie G's Livestock. Oh, and a half dozen horses. And there's paperwork on everything. The Beaumont Ranch will come alive again."

"And what about Charlie Gorwecki? Is he retiring?"

"He sure is. Lucky us. Perfect timing, isn't it?" Luke could hear the excitement in Reed's voice.

"When does the stock arrive, Reed?"

"Sometime tomorrow."

Luke whistled low. "I really appreciate what you're doing, but the barn is pretty much shot. I'll have to find another place for the horses to board or I can throw up something temporary for shelter."

"Do what you gotta do, bro. There will be more money coming your way. Jesse won the Galveston event."

"Incredible. Congratulate him for me. And thanks, partner. Thanks to you both."

"One for all—"

"And all for one!" Luke finished.

Things were moving fast. Maybe too fast. But if Charlie Gorwecki was retiring and selling out, Luke was glad to have first dibs on his stock, and it was prime Oklahoma stock since Charlie lived in Osage County.

Luke walked down the hallway, found the bathroom and hit the light. He was surprised to find a shower curtain painted with cowboy boots, dozens of them, with different logos and designs.

It made him laugh. So did the matching toothbrush holder and other accessories.

He stripped down, turned on the tap, stepped in and let the water sluice down on him. It wasn't rain, but it'd do. He lathered up with coconut-melon shampoo and mango-watermelon bath gel and thought he smelled like a fruit salad.

No wonder whenever he was around Amber, she smelled so delicious.

He pulled out a rolled-up towel from a basket on a shelf, shook it out and dried off for the second time in several minutes. Riffling through his gear bag, he found a pair of sweatpants, underwear and a T-shirt. He could sleep in that.

He ran a comb through his hair and reminded himself to get a haircut before the arena announcers and commentators made comments about his "long, wavy hair" like they had before, as if that made him a lesser bull rider.

He picked up his wet clothes and towels, and made his way to the kitchen where Amber and chocolate-chip cookies should be waiting.

As much as he liked the cookies, he was looking forward to talking with Amber again. She was a woman he could talk to.

Although she could be way too serious, she was a smart woman, and he liked that. And he liked how she loved Beaumont and how she wanted to better herself by working toward a new job. And then there was the fact that Amber appreciated how hard he worked, but she wasn't phony or overwhelming, like the stampede of buckle bunnies he inevitably had to deal with.

Amber was sitting at her kitchen table, going through her mail. Looking up, she smiled. He liked how she smiled, too. It lit up her whole face.

"Oh, your clothes. You can put them in the laundry room." She pointed to an open door on the other side of the kitchen. "There's a basket in there. Or you can put them in the washing machine if you need to do them."

"Thanks, Amber."

Luke walked to the laundry room and, from the door-way, tossed his clothes into an empty basket.

"And there's soap on the—"

He held out his hand to stop her. "I'm good. Thanks."

"Stop being so nice, Luke!"

"I *am* nice. But so are you."

"I know, but quit thanking me. Okay. Let's clear the air. Won't you sit, please?"

"Stop being so nice, Amber!" Laughing, he sat next to her. He didn't have to wait long before she pushed the plate of cookies toward him. "Are these all mine?"

"They can be. And if you ever want more, there's the cookie jar." A jar in the shape of a green cowboy boot sat on the counter next to a window with lace curtains.

"Milk, coffee or tea?" she asked, standing. "I'll get the first one, you help yourself after that."

"Milk, please," he said then snapped his fingers. "Darn. Forget I said 'please.' I meant to say, 'Fetch me milk, woman!'"

"Watch that kind of talk, cowboy," She laughed. "Remember that I have a gun…and handcuffs."

"Promises…promises."

She pushed her chair away from the table and he noticed that, along with a pink T-shirt from a breast cancer walk and run, she was wearing a pair of beige shorts. Her legs were nice to look at—tanned and strong—and she was barefoot.

If Amber looked good in cop clothes, she looked even better in street clothes.

It was strange thinking of Amber as a potential date. She was just an old acquaintance from high school. Although he knew everyone he went to school with, Amber had never been on his radar. She was just…there. He'd never thought to ask her out back then, but what about now?

"Amber, are you dating anyone? Should I watch my back if your boyfriend finds out that I'm staying with you?"

She hesitated. "I don't have a boyfriend. Your back is safe."

Now what should I say?

She placed a tall glass of milk in front of him. "Help yourself, Luke."

He reached for a cookie and sunk his teeth into the best chocolate-chip cookie he'd ever had.

"Geez, Amber, is there anything you can't do? You can bake. That's all you need!"

She laughed and sat down. "And I can even cook, too. Um, there have been boyfriends, but we never went the distance. I guess I can be a bit intimidating."

He met her gaze. "I don't think that. I think you just know what needs to be done, and you speak your mind. You spoke your mind to me at the autographing, and here I am. You also have a good heart, Amber. You do, and that means everything. And that's coming from my gut."

Dammit. Tears pooled in her spring-green eyes. He was making her cry. "Aw…don't cry. I didn't mean to make you cry."

She dabbed at her eyes with a napkin. "They're good tears."

"My mother used to say that."

Amber nodded. "And you have good memories of your mother?"

"Absolutely. And she loved the ranch. One of the reasons we are fixing it up is to honor her memory."

She put her hand over his.

He liked that. Friendship. That's what it was.

He patted her hand and she quickly removed it. "Amber, why did you become a cop?"

"You'd laugh if I told you."

"Bet I wouldn't."

She hesitated, as if thinking where to start. "As you know, my father was a moonshiner. I say *was*, because he swears that he isn't doing it anymore. Anyway, law-enforcement officers were always stopping by the house to catch him moonshining and with hot car parts. Most of the time, they weren't disappointed, but my father could talk his way out of anything. A case of 'shine here…a bribe there…a whitewall tire here. Every time they came I was scared out of my wits. And what followed was the argument between my folks because my mother hated it as much as I did. I wanted to be a cop to make my father stop."

He nodded. "Any regrets?"

"That I probably didn't make my father stop, after all, and now he has my brothers mixed up in everything."

He nodded. "I saw that stockpile of jars."

She drummed her fingers on the table. "It was hard to miss. Something's up. And I hate the fact that they are lying to me, but I'll catch them sooner or later."

They made small talk and Luke wiped out the dish of cookies. "Your couch is calling to me." He yawned. "Would you mind if I said good-night now?"

"Heavens! It's one in the morning! You've had a long, long day." She jumped up. "Let me get you some pillows and blankets."

"Thanks." Then he realized what he'd said. "I mean, get me some pillows and blankets, woman!"

She chuckled. "Come and help me, cowboy."

Another thing he liked about Amber was joking with her.

Tomorrow was going to be another busy day and he hoped that they could spend more time together.

But this relationship would have to stay purely platonic. He didn't have any time to spend on a long-term liaison. He needed to concentrate on fixing up the ranch until the PBR started back up in a couple of months. Then he was going to go for another World Finals win in November. That would be his second and would put him among the elite riders.

He'd never had any luck with a serious relationship. Or maybe, as Amber had said, he couldn't find anyone he could go the distance with.

Could he go the distance with Amber?

Chapter Eight

Amber couldn't sleep. It was hard to believe that the number-one bull rider in the world was spending the night on her couch.

He was one of *those* Beaumonts.

She was one of *those* Chapmans.

If there had been train tracks going through town, she would have been born, and grown up, on "the other side" of them.

He'd grown up in the most historical home and land in the tri-county area.

She'd grown up surrounded by a junkyard.

Amber didn't know why she was thinking about the differences between Luke and herself; she ought to be thinking about what they had in common.

High school. The same town. Only he'd left. Of course, they both liked bull riding. Oh, and they both wanted to see the Beaumont Ranch fixed up. Luke wanted it restored to honor the memory of his mother and his ancestors, and she wanted it restored because of its tourist value and because it employed a good part of the town.

At about five in the morning, she tossed on a robe and went out to the kitchen to start the coffee. Of course, the first thing her eyes settled on was the sight of Luke stretched across her couch. Sometime during the night the blankets had dropped on the floor and one of his legs was hanging off the couch. His T-shirt was off, and his sweats hung low on his flat stomach.

What a gorgeous hunk of a man!

Amber forced herself to concentrate on making coffee, but all she wanted to do was to take a seat in the living room and look at Luke until her eyes dried up like a beached trout.

He groaned and moved around in his sleep until he got comfortable. Amber hurried over to his side, picked up the blankets and gently covered him. It was like covering a work of art.

"Thanks, Amber," he mumbled.

She jumped. "No problem, cowboy. Now go back to sleep."

"I can't. Long day. Gotta…get…up." Two minutes later he started snoring.

Amber finished fixing the coffee then turned it on. Soon it started dripping and the delicious aroma permeated the air.

"Woman, how about some bacon and eggs and home fries with onions?"

"Sure, cowboy!" Amber's voice rang out. "Cereal and milk coming right up. A banana is optional."

"Cereal? For a hardworking man? The least you could do is throw in a chocolate-chip cookie."

"I can do that."

"What the hell time is it?" he asked.

"Five fifteen in the morning."

"You get up this early?"

"My sleep clock is all crazy due to the shifts I work. I guess I had enough sleep."

"I might as well get an early start on the day. Over ten stock trucks will be arriving at the ranch sometime today." He rubbed his face to wake up. "The Beaumonts will be back in business. And Big Dan Beaumont will be miserable."

"Wow! Several trucks. That's great about the stock, Luke! And don't worry about your father. He'll come around."

"Hope you're right." Luke folded the blankets and set them and the pillows on a neat pile on the couch. "Excuse me while I get dressed and tidy up," he said, heading for the bathroom with his bag.

Amber fussed with a bright, flowery tablecloth and added matching napkins. She set out bowls, milk, bananas, and poured coffee. As she was setting out the silverware, she stopped, thinking.

Maybe she would make him the bacon, eggs and home fries tomorrow. She had to make a quick trip to the store. And the number-one item on the list would be chocolate chips for more cookies.

Amber enjoyed fussing—especially for someone who appreciated it, like Luke.

He returned minutes later. His hair was combed and the waves somewhat tamped down. He had on a pair of worn jeans, a black T-shirt and an old pair of cowboy boots.

"I'm ready for work," Luke said.

"Me, too." Amber wore an old pair of paint-covered jeans, an orange T-shirt that said Oklahoma Sooners Football and a pair of black sneakers. She had her hair pulled up in a short ponytail. "I'm ready to help, but we need energy. Have a seat."

He pulled out a chair and sat. "This is really nice of you."

"It's nothing special. Granola with a banana, some juice. I should be serving protein for such a long day, but I have to stop at the grocery store."

"It's fine, Amber. And the next time, I'm buying. We can go to a breakfast place or out to dinner. Is the Egg-cellent Diner around still? How about Howie's?"

"Yes. They're still around, but my cooking is just as good as theirs."

"Of course it is," he said. "I was just saving you work." He cut up a banana into his bowl and added granola and milk.

"Yeah, well, you're being too nice again."

He beat his chest with his fists. "Restaurant. Breakfast. You and me."

"How about if we wait a couple of days? I'd like to whip up some pancakes with bacon and home fries for you. I make the best pancakes. My home fries are to die for. I load them up with onions and add my secret ingredient that isn't such a secret—dill weed."

"I haven't had a home-cooked meal since—" Turning his head, he stared out the window, as if thinking of another time, a better time. "I've had a lot of meals at a lot of restaurants, some better than others."

He didn't have to finish.

She guessed that he hadn't had a home-cooked meal since his mother died.

Since Amber loved to bake and cook, she was going to make sure she made whatever Luke liked before he had to go back on the road.

"Luke, do you like lasagna?"

"Love it." He scooped a spoonful of cereal into his mouth.

"How about baked chicken, mashed potatoes and gravy?" she asked.

"Nothing better."

She checked off her list. "Spaghetti and meatballs?"

"Yum."

"For breakfast, do you like eggs, waffles, pancakes, French toast, omelets?"

He laughed. "All at one time or separate?"

"Separate!"

"Yes times five."

"Pork chops, steak, corned beef and cabbage?"

"Yes, yes and yes."

"Let me make this simple," Amber said. "Is there anything that you don't like?"

"Off the top of my head…liver."

He took another spoonful of cereal and fished in the milk for some banana. "But, Amber, like I said, it's enough that you offered to help with the ranch. I don't expect you to cook and bake for me."

"I know. You made that clear. But I'd like to make a double batch of cookies and we can take some to your father."

"We? You mean you'd want to see Big Dan again?"

She shrugged. "Sure. I think that he's going to have a breakthrough soon. It's like the rehab of the Beaumont Ranch and at the same time the rehab of Big Dan Beaumont."

"Speaking of the ranch, do you mind if we hustled there just in case the stock trucks are early?" Luke asked.

"No problem." Amber picked up the empty bowls and put them in the dishwasher along with the silverware and their coffee mugs. She poured the extra coffee into two travel mugs and handed one to Luke.

"I could have done that, but you move so fast," he said.

"No moss grows under my feet, cowboy."

"Amber, you're like the eighth wonder of the world."

"Luke Beaumont, you haven't seen anything yet. You just watch me!"

LUKE CALLED THE only car rental in town. All they could offer him was a 1996 thirty-foot Winnebago motor home. He passed on it and decided to ask Amber's brother to look at his truck again.

They got excited as they both brainstormed things that needed to be done at the ranch and what supplies Luke needed to buy.

He jotted everything down on a yellow legal pad Amber had given him along with a Beaumont Sheriff's Department pen.

The list was getting longer and longer.

Luke read it out. "This is what I have so far. Nails for Sheetrock and plywood. Fifty two-by-fours. Sheetrock— fifty sheets to start. Six sledgehammers. Fifty sheets of 5/8 plywood. Two-by-sixes for outside walls of new shed— eighty boards. I don't know how large to make the new shed…"

"Are you going to tear the existing barn down?"

"I'll probably just tear the roof down. It's half down anyway, but the walls seem okay. We'll see what happens when I get to it. I'd like to pound out a shed to shade the horses and then add on a stable down the line. The current one looks like the Snake River."

"And after the shed?" she asked.

"The house, of course."

"You know, Luke… I was thinking. Because of the historic nature of the Beaumont homestead, you'll qualify for federal funds, but you'll have a lot of guidelines as to the materials you have to use."

"Cool. But won't it take forever?"

"Uh…no. Donna's already started on it. Donna O'Neill. She's the president of the Beaumont Historical Society, and I'm the secretary. We both did the paperwork for you, based on everything that's been written on the Beaumonts, starting with Pierre. It just needs your signature and then it's going to get the federal fast track because it's one of the top historical attractions in Oklahoma." She was so excited that she paused to catch her breath. "I hope you don't think I'm interfering."

"No. Absolutely not. I think it's great. Do you have the specs I have to follow?"

"Basically, it's a primer on how to make adobe and stucco."

"My grandfather and father taught me that when we made a pump house for the pool. Granddad wanted the area to look like the house."

"Then you're all set. You have to have Donna checking on our progress from time to time."

"Our progress? You're going to make adobe and stucco with me?"

"Sure. It'll come in handy in my police work. You never know when I'll have to make a historical jail!" she joked.

"You know, let's do a jail later. The tourists will love it!"

"Speaking of tourists, how often will there be tours through the place?"

"Tours?" Luke asked.

"Yes, just like before when your mother gave them. People love the history of the ranch." She shrugged. "That's the price of taking federal funds." Amber turned down the main Beaumont road. "It can be open a couple times a week. And you don't have to lead the tour. Someone from the historical society can be docent."

"Okay." He scribbled more items on the pad. "Let me think about it all. Oh, and here come the stock trucks."

"And here is your help." Amber pointed to a dozen men who were waiting. "While you were getting ready, I put the word out about the trailers coming in. They're going to match up each animal with their vaccination record and ancestry. Then they're going to turn them out."

He sighed. "Shoot, Amber. I can't begin to repay you. I know that you're doing it for the town and not for me because we barely know each other—"

"Even though we're living together." She chuckled.

"Yeah…even though we're living together. I really appreciate everything you've done. From my father to the tax sale to the historical grant, and everything in between. You've gone above and beyond. How can I possibly repay you?"

"I'll take tickets to the Finals in Vegas, all five days. But you have to win. Then we'll be even."

"I have to win and then we'll be even?" he repeated.

"Yes."

"That's a tall order—not the tickets, but the win."

"You can do it, Luke. You'll make history as the only rider who won two back-to-back titles."

"I'll win it for you."

"Win it for Beaumont, Oklahoma."

"Amber, whether or not you realize it, you *are* Beaumont, Oklahoma."

EARLY IN THE EVENING, the stock was all unloaded and it did Amber's heart good to see what prime horses, cattle and bulls that the Beaumont brothers had bought.

Day after day, more neighbors arrived armed with carpenter tools and tools of destruction and they proceeded to take down the barn roof. Another crew helped Luke with a smaller shed. Later, when new stalls were made, the shed would serve as a tack room and storage place. Donna O'Neill watched the progress and made suggestions to keep it historically accurate.

Amber went where needed, fetching wood and passing out sandwiches she made on a folding table she'd found in the barn, cleaned up and added a plaid, vinyl tablecloth. A cooler nearby was filled with ice and contained various kinds of soda.

In between, she worked the night shift, manning the desk at the department, and found herself wishing that she was back at the ranch. She caught some sleep when she could, and made dozens and dozens of sandwiches.

She was elated to see her family chipping in, too.

Her brother Ronnie fixed Luke's old pickup with a warning that Luke needed a new battery. Luke went back and forth to her apartment in it. Amber was working the three-to-eleven shift, so when she arrived at her place, she was greeted with Luke snoring on the couch.

The man was working nonstop. So was she, but she never felt so good. Maybe she'd take some time off from work and help Luke out more. She had a batch of unused vacation days.

Chapter Nine

Two days later, on a sunny, cool morning, Amber was helping the barn crew nail floorboards when she saw Luke approach. Judging by his slumped shoulders and the urgent way he was walking, something was wrong. "I have some cattle missing," Luke said, face flaming.

Amber set down her hammer and readied herself to duck when the steam started shooting from his ears.

"How do you know?" Amber asked.

"I just talked to Slim. He ought to know. He's the longest-running ramrod of the Beaumont Ranch. My father hired him years ago."

"Slim's a good man and he's really loyal to the Beaumonts. He'd know. Where are they missing from?"

"The northeast pasture."

Amber couldn't move, couldn't breathe. "Isn't that the pasture that runs above my father's backyard on the hill?"

"You said it. I didn't."

Amber took a deep breath. "What do you mean by that?"

"I'm not accusing anyone but—"

She shrugged. "Say it. 'But your dad and brothers have no real income.' Right, Luke?" Her mouth suddenly turned dry and she couldn't swallow. "They have the junkyard for income."

"I can't believe that the junkyard supports your father and three men. Can you?"

"Luke, let me talk to my dad before you make accusations that you'll have to take back."

"I'll be glad to take everything back if I'm wrong. Go ahead. Talk to them. I don't believe that they'll tell you anything. That's why I'm going to see Captain Fitzgerald this afternoon. Maybe he can find the rustlers."

"Luke. Wait awhile, will you?"

"I can't. If it's not stopped, more will be gone." He shook his head. "When does Captain Fitzgerald work today?"

"He's on three-to-eleven, same as me. But let me handle this."

"Are you worried that I'm right and your family might be involved?"

She didn't answer.

"Okay," Luke said. "You talk to your father. I'll talk to Captain Fitzgerald and report the theft. Maybe we'll find out what's going on."

"You already believe that it's my family that stole your cattle, but I'd like to ask you to keep an open mind."

"Open mind?" He rolled his eyes. "Where your brothers are concerned?"

"Yes."

"I never got along with your brothers in high school or the few times I've seen them after graduation. They kept calling me Prince of Beaumont, Your Majesty and that kind of thing. We were in the guidance office for fighting more than anyone."

"What you're trying to say is that you're already prejudiced against my brothers." It was the same old thing all the time. The Chapmans were guilty until proven innocent. Even Luke was quick to convict them. It had frustrated her and made her angry her whole life.

Luke took a deep breath. "Okay, okay. I'll reserve judgment and will keep my comments to myself, but I'll give you until five o'clock tonight. Then, I'll meet you at your office and we'll both talk to the captain."

Luke had some nerve blaming her brothers and/or her father for stealing cattle. Then again, she was quick to blame them, too, and without evidence.

She knew what they were like and she was the first to admit that they loved to make a quick, easy buck, but cattle rustling was way out of their league.

She raised her index finger. "The rustlers would have to find a truck to transport the cattle and find a buyer."

"Not necessarily. Maybe the buyer has a truck."

"We'll see."

If it turned out to be a Chapman who was responsible for rustling Luke's cattle, there would be no rock that they could hide under.

When she became a cop, her father had promised that he'd stay out of trouble and make sure that her brothers did, too. If they'd broken their promise, she'd hunt them down like mad dogs and see that they were behind bars.

Two hours later, after she fussed and fretted while shoveling out mud and debris from the house, she sought out Luke, who was carrying a stack of lumber on his shoulder. He was sweating and the ends of his pitch-black hair were wet and curling.

In spite of all the things on her mind, she had to admit that Luke looked sexy, but she quickly dismissed the thought. He was intent on blaming her family for the loss of his cattle and that tweaked every cell in her body.

"I'm leaving. I'm going to my father's house and see if I can find anything out about your cattle," she snapped. "There're a bunch of sandwiches in the cooler. Everyone can help themselves."

"Should I find another couch to stay on from now on?"

"I just as soon have you nearby so I can watch you eat your words."

"Okay, Amber. I know the fact that I never got along with your brothers is tainting my judgment, but I can't help myself. I want to be proven wrong. I do."

"I hope to do just that. See you later, Luke."

"Later."

CAPTAIN FITZGERALD POUNDED his fist on his desk. "Luke Beaumont just returned to Beaumont, finally. He's fixing up his disaster of a place and now he has to deal with this? Who the hell has the sand to do this to him?"

Amber's heart was pumping way too fast and her cheeks heated. She was sure the captain was thinking that the Chapmans were somehow involved.

"Luke will be here in a while. He's going to file a complaint."

"We haven't had a cattle rustling case in a decade or two. How many are missing, Sergeant?"

"Slim Gomez thinks ten."

"Slim's the best cattleman around. I'm surprised he stuck with the Beaumonts. Especially when the boys weren't around and Big Dan started drinking."

Amber nodded. "I'd like to be assigned the investigation, Captain."

"Uh… Amber, I don't know. I just don't know. Maybe Mike Dolan—"

"Captain, I will be neutral and impartial and will find the perps, no matter who they are."

Today, and every day, she didn't like her professionalism as a law-enforcement officer questioned. The cap should know her work by now.

"Okay, Amber. Let's see what you can do on this case. But if you are, uh… If you find yourself, um, in a jam…"

"I'll discuss it with you, Cap." And she would. Even though he gave her the assignments that no one wanted, she trusted his advice.

"Good, Sergeant. So you have any idea where to start?"

"I'll start with Slim Gomez. Then I'm going to check for truck tracks somewhere in or around the pasture where they were turned out."

The door swung open and Amber spun around.

Luke.

"Hello again, Amber. Hello, Captain."

"Well, Luke Beaumont! It's been a long time, but I've been following your career. My money's on you to win the Finals."

He chuckled. "Thanks, Captain. I'll do my best, so you won't lose your bet."

"Amber was just telling me about your missing cattle," Captain Fitzgerald said.

"They aren't missing. They were rustled. I'd like to report the incident."

"Sure. Sergeant Chapman will take your statement. I've already assigned her to the case," Captain Fitzgerald said, twirling a pen in his hand.

"Uh…you've assigned her to the case?"

The captain nodded.

"Captain, can I speak to you in private?" Luke asked.

Amber knew why he was asking and she fumed. Luke was sidelining her, just like Fitz usually did.

"If you have any concern about my fitness to handle your case, then you can speak in front of me."

He winked. "Not if I need a place to stay!"

The captain raised an eyebrow and his eyes grew big.

On another day the shocked expression on the captain's face would have made her laugh. But not today.

"It's not what you think," Amber said then turned to Luke. "Say what you have to say."

"If your family is involved, are you able to turn them in?"

Amber took a deep breath. "I told you before I could."

Luke shifted on his booted feet. At least he had the sense to be uncomfortable. "I want to hear it again. In front of the captain."

"I would arrest them in the same amount of time, or less, that it takes you to ride a bull. Eight seconds. Now let's end this. The CIA has less screening."

"I'm satisfied," Luke said.

"Me, too." Captain Fitzgerald said.

"Finally." Amber knew that the captain would watch her like a hawk and question her judgment until the perps were arrested and convicted.

"Luke, I'd like to borrow one of your horses and check out your northeast pasture," she said.

"They're all new to me. I believe that a couple of them are tame and broken for riding, but most are rodeo stock. I'll have to ask Slim to get two ready."

"Two? I can only ride one at a time."

Oh, no. He wouldn't dare. He just wouldn't dare!

"I'm going with you." He dared.

"Captain, this is an official investigation of the Beaumont County Sheriff's Department."

"But you just asked Luke to loan you a horse." The two men made eye contact. "He just wants to make sure you're treating his animal okay."

She saw the wink from the captain to Luke. Soon they were going to run toward each other and bump stomachs.

"Captain, I must protest—" Amber began.

"Duly noted."

Ah...yes. The Good Ole Boys network.

Another reason why she couldn't wait to join the state police.

"Now, you both just excuse me. I have an appointment with Mayor Kendall." He picked up his cowboy hat, slapped it on his head, gave it a tap, which he did for good luck, and was gone.

She turned to Luke. "Don't even think about going with me."

"Don't even think of keeping me away. Two heads are better than one. Besides, I have a stake in finding my cattle."

"So do I, Luke. So do I."

You have no idea.

Luke checked his watch. "Amber, would you like to have dinner with me? Today would be perfect to treat you for all the wonderful meals you've been making, and the sandwiches you've been passing out for everyone at lunch."

"I don't need any repayment, so thank you for thinking of me, but I'd like to get started on the investigation tonight. Maybe talk to Slim. But I bought the fixings for a meatloaf and a salad for us for dinner."

"Amber, I'm surprised that I haven't worn out my welcome and you're still feeding me and letting me back on your couch."

"Maybe I'm kind of getting used to you on my couch, and I do like cooking for you. You're very appreciative."

"Since I'm on the road a lot working the circuit and eating every meal out, your cooking is heaven. It's just like—"

"Your mother used to make."

He smiled slightly but his eyes dimmed. "Yes."

"I like going out, but I like cooking better. Let's do that meatloaf. While it's cooking we can—"

"Talk about the investigation?" Luke asked.

"Clean out my spare bedroom so you can move in there."

"That's just what I meant." He winked. "One more favor?"

She put her hands on her hips as if she was thinking about it, but she knew he needed a ride, and she wasn't going to make it easy for him. He was beginning to take advantage of her. "It depends."

"Give me a ride to your house. My pickup didn't start again and wouldn't take a charge," Luke said. "I guess I have to spring for a new battery. Your brother said that it was time, but I haven't had a chance to get one."

"How did you get here? And don't tell me that you hitchhiked."

"Okay I won't. I could have bummed a ride, but I didn't want to take anyone off the job. It was Matty Matthews who picked me up. He was going to visit my father as he had to do an updated report to the court. Matty said that Dad is doing okay. He won't participate in group counseling, but he's okay one-on-one with Matty and another counselor there."

"That's great, Luke. I bet you are relieved."

"Relieved is right, but I'm still holding my breath because by now he knows that we have stock—a lot of stock—and he knows that a lot of people are helping to rebuild the ranch. It's all happening without his approval and without him. This won't be good for his treatment progress, and that's what I told Matty."

"Do you want to visit him? I'll drive you over. This time I'll wait for you either in my car or in the lobby."

"Thanks, but I'm beat. I'll visit him tomorrow for sure. I'll look into renting a car, so I'm not imposing on you until your brother can take another look at my truck."

"Good. Tomorrow I'm going to immerse myself in your case. You'll be busy working and visiting Big Dan."

"I hired a professional roofing company to do the barn roof. They have the specialized equipment. They're starting tomorrow. I couldn't expect the volunteers to tackle that job."

"That's good. You can do something else that needs your attention."

"What needs my attention is my missing stock. And I'll have the time to saddle up two horses and to help you. What a lucky break, huh?"

"Gee, how lucky can I get? But, Luke, if I wanted a partner, I could have asked for one. Truth is, I work better alone."

Who was she kidding? She worked alone because none of the cavemen that she worked with wanted to partner with her. If she heard one more "you might break a nail doing real cop work" or the like, she was going to scream at them. Well, she had on several occasions. That hadn't worked, so she'd spoken softly. She'd spoken nicely. She'd baked up a storm. She'd regularly bought doughnuts and supplied coffee. She'd used humor, briefly, she'd tried being one of the guys. Nothing had worked.

They didn't want it to work.

Chief Fitz just wanted peace. Even though she didn't like some of the things he did, she respected his position, so she gave him peace and didn't complain.

Not much, anyway.

Amber waved goodbye to the dispatcher who was working behind a big glass window, surrounded by several desktop computers and various maps of Beaumont County on the wall.

Luke looked shocked that they hadn't been alone.

"Right now, all the guys who are on duty are in the field. There's always a dispatcher," she explained.

"Let's go home, then. Um, I mean to your house."

It warmed Amber's heart that Luke had thought of her apartment as "home" before he'd corrected himself. She supposed that it was much different than what he'd been used to over the last few years—and what he was used to were hotel rooms.

As they walked to Amber's car she felt boneless and fuzzy inside.

She hadn't felt like that since she was eight and gotten the present she'd wanted for her birthday—Teenage Tara Turner and her condo. When she'd opened the pink plastic carrying case, there was Tara and her magnificent pink house.

She was glad that Luke felt comfortable at her place. It was cozy and comfortable, and it begged for a couple of kids running around.

Amber had thought about kids occasionally, but this

was the first time she pictured Luke there playing with her dream children.

He'd be a great dad.

Huh? Kids? Luke as a dad! Where was her head?

She was a cop and, with any luck, she was soon to be a state police officer, and would be moving from her cute apartment over the Happy Tea Pot. Luke would go back on the road with the Professional Bull Riders.

She didn't have a future with Luke.

For that matter, she didn't have a future with anyone.

Tears pooled in her eyes and she blinked them back—all except for one errant tear that ran down her cheek. She brushed it away with a finger.

"Amber, are you crying?"

Four more steps and she would have been in her car, facing the road, and Luke would never have caught her crying.

She sniffed. "Negative. Something's in my eye. An eyelash, maybe."

"Let me have a look."

He took both her arms and stood in front of her, so that she had to face him.

His blue eyes studied her face. "You *are* crying."

"It's nothing, really. Something just hit me and got me thinking. It's gone now. Let's get moving."

She always got weepy when she thought she'd never have children. With her three shifts and constant over-time, finding a babysitter would be a nightmare anyway.

See? Impossible.

Another tear escaped and she turned away.

Luke wasn't easy to shake. "What's wrong, Amber? Did I say something to hurt you?"

"Of course not." She shook her head. "Let's go."

Luke held on to her upper arms and searched her face as if her reason for her meltdown was inked on her face.

It would be so easy to step into his arms, just to lay her head on his chest for a while or to get a warm hug.

Instead, Luke gently held her face in his hands and kissed her forehead. It was so tender, she almost cried again.

"I hate it when women cry, especially you, Amber. You're such a strong woman, something must be really bothering you."

"I can't tell you. Not right now, Luke. I will someday if the occasion presents itself."

He bent his head and kissed her lips—softly, lightly. "I'll wait until you're ready."

When he stopped, she wanted to scream. Then his lips closed over hers again and it was just like her dreams, only much, much better. With each kiss, she knew she'd never be the same again.

Chapter Ten

The next day, Amber was walking on sunshine. Her stomach fluttered whenever she thought of Luke's kisses. It felt comfortable sitting with Luke in her kitchen. She was reading the paper while Luke was looking at his cell phone and drinking coffee, he let out a deep breath and shouted, "I forgot all about it!"

"Forgot about what?" Amber asked.

"The Bull Riders' Ball. Because I'm the reigning world champion, they asked me to be master of ceremonies and I agreed. It's tomorrow night in Pueblo, Colorado."

"Did you get a plane ticket?" Amber asked.

"Nope. It completely escaped my mind. I'll get two tickets on the first plane out of here tomorrow."

Amber wondered who he was taking with him. Her stomach sank.

"That is...would you go with me to the Bull Riders' Ball, Amber?"

"I'd love to go!"

"I'll get a hotel, too. We'll probably have to stay over one night. The ball is at night. Oh, and it's formal. I'd better rent a tux." He checked his watch. "Where should I go?"

"The Beaumont Tux Rental. It's on First Street. You

can't miss it. It's in between Beaumont Bowling Lanes and Beaumont Bakery." She laughed. Everything in Beaumont was Beaumont This or Beaumont That.

"I have to go shopping," Amber said. "It's not as if I have a ball gown hanging in my closet." In fact, her last long dress had been for the senior prom!

Luke chuckled. "Why don't we go together? We can grab some lunch, too."

Amber wanted to pick out a fabulous dress and she didn't want Luke to see it until the night of the Bull Riders' Ball.

"Let's go separately. I'll drop you off and we can go to lunch. I'll pick you up about one thirty. I'd like to take you to—"

He snapped his fingers. "Smokin' Sammy's House of Hickory?"

"The Happy Tea Pot and China Shop. It's open now. I've always wanted to go there. It's right below my apartment and I've never stopped there. I'll call and make a reservation. How about two o'clock?"

"I can't wait," he said sarcastically, but his eyes were twinkling. Luke Beaumont was a good sport.

Amber grinned. "Okay. See you at one thirty."

SHE PARKED IN FRONT of the house and sighed when she noticed a new collection of hubcaps on the porch.

Finding no one at home, she let herself in and went to her old bedroom at her parents' house. She had to know if her senior prom dress would fit her and if it was still in style.

She didn't know why she wanted to try it on, but she'd barely had time to wear it before Crazy Kenny had shot off his drunken mouth and hurt her intensely.

Amber thought back to her prom.

She had wished every day during senior year that Luke would ask her. But he never had. When Amber had heard that he'd asked Lacy Stevens, she'd been devastated. When Kenny Fowler had asked her to the prom, she'd said yes out of desperation.

Taking the dress out of the closet, she looked at it on the hanger. It was a very pretty light blue chiffon with a touch of sparkle in the fabric. The bodice crisscrossed her breasts and she remembered how it fell in a gentle circle at her feet.

She'd worked hard at Beaumont Pizza for the dress and saved every penny of her minimum-wage paycheck.

And she'd worn it for roughly an hour.

Slipping it over her head, she held her breath. It was just wishful thinking that it would fit.

It didn't. It was too tight in the chest and too short. But it was just an impulse. Now she knew the type of gown she was going to buy.

It was just a short trip to Beaumont Formals, which had the same style in her size but in a flaming red.

Instead she went for a slinky black dress with a fairly plunging neckline and crystal beads on the bodice. Bonnie Douglas, a self-proclaimed stylist, insisted that "Luke Beaumont's eyeballs would fall right out of his head in eight seconds" at the Bull Riders' Ball.

Sold!

She had great shoes to wear with it. Jewelry that would be perfect. She was all set and couldn't wait to see Luke's eyeballs hit the ground in eight seconds when he saw her in that dress.

That would be her fantasy come true.

WHEN LUKE FIRST walked into the Happy Tea Pot, it was like another era. He was overwhelmed by all the teacups and saucers on display.

The curtains were lace. The sofa and chairs were upholstered with cabbage roses, as was the owner's dress.

"Mrs. Prestin, do you know Luke Beaumont?" Amber asked.

"Of course. Who doesn't know Luke? But what I'd like to know, Luke, is why you haven't been in my shop before now."

Mrs. Prestin wore a maid's apron that was right out of *Downton Abbey* and it sounded like she was faking a British accent.

Luke nodded. "I haven't been home much, Mrs. Prestin, but I'm here now and I'd like to experience high tea."

"Pardon my nosiness, but are you two a couple? You and Amber?" Mrs. Prestin leaned forward as if the answer was going to be the juiciest piece of gossip since Reverend Maloney had bought a Ferrari with church funds.

Luke pushed his cowboy hat back with a thumb. "You know, Mrs. Prestin, I'd like you to be the first to know that yes, we are a couple, but we're trying to keep it quiet."

He took Amber's hand and kissed the back of it.

"And we're living together," Amber added, playing around. She gave Luke a kiss on the cheek.

"Oh! Oh, my!" Mrs. Prestin said. "Let me show you to a table."

They sat on a couch fronted by a low table covered with a lace tablecloth. They were handed a menu describing what they'd be having.

Then Mrs. Prestin waddled off. Luke saw her on the

phone, no doubt spreading the word that Amber Chapman and Luke Beaumont were a "couple."

"My name is Jill and I will be your hostess to many of our special courses. First, our tea of the day is jasmine," said Jill, who didn't bother with a British accent. However, she wore a type of doily on her head with two ribbons hanging down in the back, a black uniform and a white apron.

"Isn't jasmine a flower?" Luke asked.

The waitress curtsied. "Yeah. Do ya still want it?"

"Why are you speaking like that, Jill? Enunciate! I told you about that before. Several times. If you don't want to work at a classy place like this, go to Beaumont Breakfast and Burgers."

Amber looked at Luke.

Luke raised an eyebrow. "We understood Jill perfectly, Mrs. Prestin. No sense putting on airs when you're not really British."

Jill smiled. "Jasmine tea is fine, Jill."

"And here is our menu, Luke…I mean Mr. Beaumont. I watch you riding all the time on TV. You are really the best."

"Jill! Our customers do not want to listen to your incessant babbling. You are here to wait on them and nothing more. Remember, you are supposed to blend into the background."

A blush started on Jill's neck and before the lecture was done it had reached her cheeks.

"Mrs. Prestin," Amber said, butting in. She just couldn't help herself. "I realize that you are new to Beaumont and the Happy Tea Pot hasn't been open very long, but if you continue to treat Jill like a rented mule, you won't have a customer in the place…ever. Word gets around, as you well know. Small-town gossips, you know."

"Well, I never—" Mrs. Prestin waddled away, the cabbage roses so tight across her butt they looked like squinted eyes.

Jill giggled. "She's going to be unbearable now, but thank you. She doesn't know it yet, but I am giving my two weeks' notice today."

"Where are you going to be working, Jill?" Luke asked.

She giggled louder. "Beaumont Breakfast and Burgers!"

"You'll like it there," Amber said. "It's down to earth and is always packed. Good tips for you."

From a corner of the room, Mrs. Prestin loudly cleared her throat. Jill jumped.

"Here's our food menu. I mean…here is our com… comp…compendium of our delightful high tea delights."

Luke took the menu and read it. "Lentil-rutabaga soup with basil, cucumber slices on toast points, clotted cream and shortbread, kale cheese curd and…boy, howdy… cherry tomatoes stuffed with couscous. Be still my heart. Can I get a cheeseburger here?"

"No, but you'll love the salmon crisps." Amber laughed.

"Oh, absolutely! I hear they're a dream with onion dip."

The rest of their time at the Happy Tea Pot went on the same vein. Amber had never laughed so much in her life. While she really enjoyed the experience with Luke, she knew it would have to come to an end.

Luke gave Jill a hefty tip and she gushed over him and his bull riding again.

"See you at Beaumont Breakfast and Burgers," Jill whispered.

"I'll look for you."

As they were walking out, Amber took Luke's hand. "Thanks for coming with me, Luke. I know it's not your thing, but you were really a good sport."

"Just as long as you liked it," he said.

"I did."

"Then it was worth it. I particularly enjoyed the flower floating in the tea."

"The edible orchid?"

"Delicious. It was the best part of high tea other than verbally sparring with Mrs. Prestin, faux British aristocrat."

She laughed. "Thanks again."

"And I particularly liked how you handled Mrs. Prestin and stuck up for Jill. I enjoyed that immensely. You're quite a woman, Amber."

Quite a woman. She basked in the glow of his compliments.

Luke squeezed her hand. "I get to pick our next date."

Date? Was she really dating Luke?

THE NEXT MORNING, Luke and Amber checked into adjoining rooms on the eighteenth floor at the Pueblo Grand Hotel and got dressed in "casual Western attire" for the welcome reception.

They almost dressed alike, but Amber wore a pink-checked blouse and Luke wore plaid. Amber had a white cowboy hat. Luke's was black.

Amber was introduced to the whole roster of bull riders—former and current—who rode with Luke.

Amber could tell that they all respected Luke, not

only because he was the previous year's champion, but because he shared his knowledge with his competitors, giving them tips and advice when asked.

Then Luke asked her to dance.

It was a slow dance, a country tune, and it felt natural to walk into Luke's arms. It felt like she was floating on air. When Luke quietly sang the words in his low, husky voice, her knees almost buckled.

When the dance ended, he was about to kiss her, but a group of young women came over to Luke with pen and program in hand. "Please, Luke. Will you sign my program?"

Two security workers hurried over. "Mr. Beaumont, are these ladies bothering you?" asked one.

"No. They're fine." Luke wrote on program after program, and Amber could tell that the girls were one step away from swooning. She could tell because she was the absolute expert on that. Only these days she was more dignified.

"Who are you, lady?" one of them asked. She had big, curly, red hair flowing down her back. It looked great on her.

"I'm Amber Chapman, Mr. Beaumont's date." She was suddenly feeling old compared to these young girls.

As if on a rescue mission, Luke put his arm around her waist. "Thanks for asking for my autograph, ladies. Now if you all will excuse me, I'm going to dance with Amber."

Luke had a way of making her feel like she was special. Before she had a chance of reveling in the feeling, he whirled her onto the dance floor. The cowboy liked to boot scoot.

By the time the welcome party was over, she felt like

she had just attended a five-hour exercise class. She didn't need Marco's Fit-nasium when she was dating Luke Beaumont!

None too soon, the event was over. "Luke, would you mind taking a walk around the block? I need some air. Or I could go myself. I don't mind."

"I'll go with you."

He took her hand and she felt euphoric, excited. Then the more they walked, it turned into quiet joy. She just loved being with Luke.

The perfect August evening was interrupted by yelling on the corner across the street.

"I'm going to get you for that, you bastard."

"Not if I get you first."

Punches were thrown and Amber could hear the unmistakable sound of flesh hitting flesh. She just had a knee-jerk reaction to trouble. When trouble presented itself, she presented herself. That was her job.

She took off running. Luke followed after her.

"Dammit, Amber! What are you doing?"

"I'm going to break up a fight."

"You can't be serious! This isn't your jurisdiction. We're in Colorado, remember?"

"Oh, yeah. I forgot," she said. "Oh, well, too late now."

"I'll watch your back," Luke said.

"Knock it off, you two!" Amber yelled. "Dammit. Stop it."

Amber realized that Luke was right. She didn't have any jurisdiction here, didn't have ID or a gun if things turned bad.

Much to her surprise, the two stopped fighting.

"What's with you, sweet thing?" one asked, looking her up and down.

"I hate to see anyone fight. Can't you just talk out your problem over a cold one instead of beating each other up?"

Luke was so close to her side she could feel the heat from his arm next to hers.

"Okay. Now shake hands and walk away before the cops come," Amber said.

"You are one hot chick," said one of the guys. "And I dig that dress."

"And she's mine," Luke said through gritted teeth.

Now that *was cool!*

Luke and Amber walked back toward the hotel. When they were away from the two, Luke said, "Amber, what were you thinking?"

She laughed. "Habit."

Luke pushed his hat back with a thumb. "She directs traffic, makes arrests, fixes up ranches and breaks up fights in another state… What else do you do, Amber?"

"I can dance," she said, feeling like flirting. "So, I think I'll go back to my room and get ready for the dance tonight."

She wanted to knock his boots off.

INSTEAD OF KNOCKING on the adjoining door that night, Luke went around to the hallway and knocked on the front door to Amber's room.

"Just a minute," he heard from inside.

He stood holding a pink tea rose corsage he'd had made in the flower shop downstairs. The clerk had assured him that Amber would love it.

When she opened the door, he felt like he'd been kicked in the ass by a twenty-one-hundred-pound bull.

"Amber, you look beautiful," he said.

"Thanks. You are looking mighty handsome tonight yourself, cowboy."

Amber was gorgeous and then some. Her blond hair fell in gentle waves to her shoulders and that black dress…damn! She looked hot! And elegant at the same time. He was speechless.

"What do you have there?" she asked as he stood in the hallway with his mouth open, corsage box in hand.

He handed it to her. "Happy senior prom."

Tears shone in Amber's eyes. "Senior prom?"

"Yes. I'd like to recreate the prom that you'd never had, if you don't mind. But if you arrived at the gym in that dress, Mrs. Maloney would have made you wear a football jersey over it, like she did with a couple of the girls back then."

Amber laughed. "I suppose the girls loved it. We all tried to push the envelope between good taste and showing a lot of skin. If Mrs. Maloney made you cover up with a football jersey, it was a great dress."

"It's a great dress, Amber. Believe me."

She grinned. "Come in, Luke. Would you mind helping me with the corsage?"

He fumbled with opening the box, pricked his finger on a long pin, but ignored it. He didn't remember fumbling like this at his real prom. For heaven's sake, he was an adult, not a testosterone-crazed high-schooler.

Amber seemed poised, the exact opposite of how he was acting. She was cool and collected in her gown with the plunging neckline and sparkling jewelry.

And he was sweating.

"Pins. Careful." Luke handed Amber the corsage. Then he pulled out the royal blue satin handkerchief from his outside pocket the tuxedo rental place had included, probably for show only. He blotted the blood from his thumb.

"Aren't you going to help me pin it on?"

"I'd rather ride a bull than tackle that treacherous thing." His eyes twinkled in merriment.

"I'll show you." She took the pins out of the corsage and held them. "Now take it and slip your hand under the fabric of my dress."

"Seriously?"

"Totally."

This was getting good. He did as she instructed, and could feel the warmth of a breast under his knuckles.

"Now take one of the big pins, hold it by the top, and slide the pin into both the fabric and some of the corsage."

He tried but got cold feet at the last minute. "I'm afraid that I'm going to stab you."

"You won't, Luke, but it can be tricky. I'll take care of it." She walked over to the mirrored closet door and pinned on the corsage with little effort.

Luke pulled out the blue handkerchief, wiped the sweat from his upper lip and mumbled, "Thank goodness."

He should have just given her a wrist corsage and slipped it on instead of putting himself through puberty again.

But above all, he wondered if he were losing it. He'd never been this idiotic around a woman before. Never.

What was Amber Chapman doing to him?

"Shall we go?" she asked, letting some kind of sparkly fabric shake out into a triangle, then handing it to him.

Oh, it was a shawl.

Luke didn't know anyone who wore one, but when he wrapped it around her shoulders and saw how it made her look even hotter in her dress, he wished she'd never take either off. Then he wished she would.

He couldn't wait to show her off in front of his fellow bull riders and everyone else. "Let's go."

They only had to go to one of the conference rooms in the hotel, so they took the elevator to the second floor. He couldn't resist, he kissed her. He kissed her from the eighteenth floor to the second floor, and it was heaven.

He teased her lips with his tongue, and she opened her mouth for him. He could hear her sigh of pleasure, and he felt invincible, and yet vulnerable.

He might be setting himself up for a relationship that wouldn't work.

When the doors opened, his brothers were standing in the hallway and he wished he had the time to get out his cell phone, find the video setting and shoot fast enough to capture their jaws dropping.

"Jesse… Reed. Hello!" he said, walking out, his hand holding on to Amber's. With everything going on, he'd forgotten that his brothers would be attending.

"Aren't you going to introduce us to your lovely lady?" Reed asked.

"You both know Amber Chapman, don't you?" Luke asked. "Amber, these are Jesse and Reed, my brothers."

She held out her hand and they both shook.

"Amber Chapman?" Jesse asked. "Wow."

"I agree with that assessment," Reed added. "Amber, I never would have recognized you."

"Thanks for everything you've done to help our father and the ranch," Jesse said. "Luke has been keeping us informed."

Reed winked. "And he's also told us that he's been living with you."

Amber winked back. "It's only because the hotels around Beaumont were full."

Jesse laughed. "Who told you that? Luke?"

A very tall man approached and tugged at the brim of his hat to Amber. "Excuse me, everyone, but, Luke, you're scheduled to go on soon."

He gave Amber's hand a squeeze. "Not without a dance first. Shall we?"

"Let's go," Amber said. "See you later, gentlemen. I'm about to be swept off my feet."

"Nah. My brother will probably step on them instead," Jesse said.

"Save a dance for me, Amber," Reed said.

"Me, too," Jesse said.

Luke sent them a dirty look. "When bulls fly, brothers."

"I HAD A great time, Luke. The best." Her throbbing feet felt like she'd danced with the top forty-five bull riders and the entire PBR staff.

She was the belle of the ball. She looked good. She felt good. If she had one complaint, it would be that she hadn't danced with Luke enough.

When she stepped into his arms, it felt as if she was safe and comfortable yet she was overflowing with joy and excitement.

Luke brought out myriad feelings within her. He always had.

She'd never forget this weekend, yet she was looking forward to getting back to Beaumont.

Even Cinderella had to find out what was going to happen next.

Chapter Eleven

As they drove home from the airport, Luke thought of how Amber had him roped and tied like a steer at a rodeo.

He wanted to make out in the car with her, but he didn't dare. It would lead to more, and Amber deserved better than sex in the front seat of her car, although there was more room in the back seat, but if they folded the back seats down...um, no.

It was for the better that he'd stopped kissing her. He was getting in over his head, but boy howdy, her perfume smelled great. Sort of like roses.

They really didn't have anything in common other than a love of bull riding and of the town of Beaumont.

Maybe not even that. They both were leaving Beaumont. He'd be going back on the road at the end of summer to get enough points for the Finals and, sooner or later, Amber would leave work for the state police somewhere.

He'd have to think on this one.

From the time she'd driven up to meet him at his autographing to the historical properties grant and even pitching in to help him, Amber had been terrific. Even before all that, she'd given Big Dan two occasions to straighten out. Even when he was arrested a third time, she'd recommended probation and rehab. Now she was driving Luke around Beaumont as if she were his personal taxi.

Amber was nice. Damn nice.

He knew a lot of nice women, but why was Amber the one he couldn't get out of his mind? Why was she the one he wanted to be with?

What puzzled him was why hadn't she kicked him out? Instead they were going to clear out a spare bedroom and she was going to make a meatloaf.

And he was liking every minute, even when they disagreed.

Amber pulled into her parking spot at the Happy Tea Pot.

"Luke, while I'm putting the meatloaf together, how about if I show you the spare room and you can tell me what can stay and what you want to go? I have a sewing machine there, a desk, a bunch of clothes stacked on the bed—just put them in my room, if you don't mind."

"I don't mind at all and, really, your couch is fine."

"Not when I come home early in the morning or have to leave early in the morning. Next week, I'm working four to midnight, so that won't be bad, but I'd hate to wake you."

Yeah, she was too nice.

"Thanks for thinking of me, but I'm the moocher. I don't want to put you out any more than I already have."

"It's no problem, and I actually enjoy cooking and baking for someone. After all, when my mother left my father, I cooked and baked for my father and brothers. I guess I'm a nurturer."

"A nurturer and a cop. Now that's interesting," Luke said.

"I think they go together."

"You're right. You got my father into rehab."

They climbed the stairs to her apartment and, after she unlocked the door, Amber headed for the kitchen. She put on a red apron that said Kiss the Cook. Luke was tempted. He'd rather kiss the cook anytime than move clothes.

"You know where the extra bedroom is, right?" Amber asked, her face in the fridge.

"Yep. The room opposite the bathroom."

"Uh-huh."

Luke went into the room. It was fine. Everything could stay. He wouldn't be there that long. Just until some hotel rooms opened up, or if he finished a room in the ranch.

He liked playing house with Amber.

But that's all it was—playing.

He moved her clothes to her bedroom like she said and called out, "What else?"

"Move the sewing machine and the cabinet to my room, too."

"Not necessary." He went to the kitchen. "Amber, the rest can stay. It's not going to bother me. I won't be here that long."

A slight frown appeared on her face and then disappeared just as fast. But he'd seen it just the same. Could it be that Amber wanted him around?

But he had to go back to the PBR. He couldn't miss the opportunity to ride every weekend and get points to keep his number-one standing. He also had to replenish his money. His bank account was looking anemic.

He stood for a while in her room. It was very nicely decorated. But…wait…she needed a closet. Going back to the kitchen, he took her hand and led her toward her bedroom. She hesitated at first, but he stated, "This won't take long."

"It won't take long?" she echoed, but it was more like a question, unlike his statement.

He noticed how red her cheeks and nose had become. It was a brilliant red.

"It's not what you think," he explained. "If we were going to make love, you'd certainly know it."

That relaxed her and she went with him. He pointed. "Right there, Amber. I could build you a closet the length of this room and some shelves inside the closet for your things."

"Don't you have enough to do?" she asked.

"How about if I build it before I'm ready to leave for the PBR? Everything should be done or on its way to being done. Okay? It'll be…uh…like paying you back for letting me crash here."

"I don't want—"

"Any payback. Yeah, I know. You said that before."

"I was going to say that I don't want you to bother. I should be moving soon."

"Oh?"

"Yes. I received a call from the state police. They asked me if I would mind being hired provisionally until I take the test and the list comes out. I jumped at it."

"And you have to move?"

"To one of the northern counties. Apparently, they need to fill some vacancies in staffing and they got a waiver from Civil Service to hire."

"Aren't you going to miss Beaumont?" he asked.

"Probably every day of my life, but I have to go for my own job satisfaction."

"I understand, Amber, I really do. But it's too bad that you have to leave. Beaumont County will miss you."

Luke helped Amber change the linens on the bed then

they made small talk in the living room. Almost two hours later, when Luke's stomach was meeting his backbone, Amber finally announced that dinner was ready.

Luke just about ran to the kitchen. "Can I help you with anything?"

He put out carrots, mashed potatoes, some kind of dark gravy, applesauce that looked homemade and, finally, the meatloaf.

Just as he picked up a fork, Luke's phone rang.

"Hello?"

"This is Marylou Haber from the Beaumont County Alcohol and Drug Rehabilitation Facility. Am I speaking to Luke Beaumont?"

"Yes. You are. What did my father do this time?" Luke asked.

"Uh…no…nothing. He's being transported by ambulance to Beaumont General. We believe he's had a heart attack."

"Oh! I'll be right there. Thanks for letting me know."

"Goodbye, Mr. Beaumont."

"Bye." He tapped off the phone and stood. He heart was thumping in double time, and he felt sick to his stomach. "I'm sorry, Amber, I have to leave. My dad had a heart attack. They're transporting him to Beaumont General by ambulance."

"Oh, I'm so sorry, Luke. Would you like me to go with you?"

"You don't have to." But he wished like hell that she'd come. She was a calming influence on him. He already lost his mother—he didn't want to lose his dad.

She stood and began stuffing the delicious meal into the fridge. "I want to go with you."

It didn't take her any time at all. Soon they were back in her SUV and she floored it.

At the corner of Carlton and Burke drives, she slowed. The ambulance had pulled over, and its lights were dim compared to what they should be like. Several people had gathered and one was shouting into his cell phone.

"Why is that ambulance stopped?" she asked, getting out of her car and running to the scene.

He followed her.

"What's going on, Craig?" she asked the ambulance driver, who stopped pacing long enough to talk to her.

"This relic finally gave up the ghost. I told the town board that we need a new one, but they don't listen."

"Where's my father?" Luke asked as he joined them.

"Don't worry. He's in the back and he's stabilized. I'm waiting for Donny Cushman to come and we'll move Big Dan."

"To his hearse?" Amber asked.

"A hearse?" Luke yelled. "Isn't that a little premature?"

"Donny's authorized to back up the ambulance. Besides, the cot is too long for a regular car and no one seems to have a big, empty van without seats. So we use Donny's hearse when the town's ambulance breaks down."

As if on cue, Donny Cushman of the Silent Repose Funeral Home arrived. The hearse gave Luke the willies.

Craig opened the back door of the ambulance. "If you have a better idea, I'm listening."

Luke didn't know what to do with his hands. "I don't. Let's go. I'll help with the stretcher or whatever it's called."

Big Dan weighed in. "Isn't this something? An ambulance that breaks down? Why doesn't this darn town have a decent one?"

"Calm down, Big Dan," Amber said. "Things are under control. You're going to be transferred to this, um, hearse."

"I ain't dead, dammit!"

"Look, Dad. Donny Cushman gave up his time to help you. So calm down and we'll get you to the hospital."

Amber was directing traffic. "Get moving!" she yelled from the middle of the intersection. "Get Big Dan into the hearse."

She went into full cop mode, yelling at the rubber-neckers to move along. He didn't like to see her in the dark and without a flashlight or her uniform on.

Luke jogged over to Amber. "I'm going in the hearse with my father," Luke said. "Meet you at the hospital?"

"Okay." She nodded, waving a dark vehicle on. "Meet you there."

Luke helped the EMTs slide his father into the back of the hearse. He hoped this wasn't an omen.

"I'm all right. Get me out of this death box on wheels."

"Calm down, Big Dan. We'll be at the hospital in ten minutes," said Donny. "And my vehicle is not a death box on wheels. It's a state-of-the-art easy rider."

"Easy rider? Who are you kidding?" Dan said.

They all chose to ignore Dan's comments, but it was ten minutes of hell driving to the hospital, with him whining and complaining ad nauseam.

Luke calmed him down by talking about PBR stats and how his two brothers were doing. He avoided telling him about the missing cattle, but the word would be out soon. Small town.

Luke took his father's hand. "Dad, just think of all the things you have to live for and quit being so cranky."

There was quiet, at least for a while.

Luke sat back in the front seat and zoned out for a minute or two. He couldn't get Amber out of his mind. She really was a skilled cop, and a skilled cook, and a skilled baker.

And she certainly could kiss.

Finally, Craig pulled into the hospital's emergency room entrance area.

"We're just using this because the ambulance broke down again," Craig yelled to waiting staff.

Luke sprang out of the hearse, but was pushed aside by hospital personnel. He let them do what they were best at and he followed the stretcher into the ER.

Funny how things worked out. If anyone ever told him five years ago that Big Dan would have a heart attack, he'd never believe it.

He used to be a robust guy, a boisterous, happy guy— the exact opposite of what he was now.

Big Dan was still boisterous, but not in a good way.

"Luke, get me out of this hospital. I don't want to spend one more minute here than I have to."

"You might have to stay overnight," Luke said and immediately regretted it.

Big Dan swore loudly. "I don't need no damn hospital. Just have them get me some pills and cut me loose."

"Calm down, Dad. And be quiet, will you? These people are trying to help you."

He was poked and prodded, and on occasion Luke tried not to laugh at his father's reaction. On other times, he couldn't help but remember how Big Dan used to be— an amiable guy who never met a person he didn't like.

Now he was just an ill-tempered crank, and it broke Luke's heart. Maybe with enough therapy, his father might return to the man he used to be.

They got him a room in record time to probably shut him up so he wouldn't disturb the rest of the patients.

After a while, Luke heard knocking and turned to find Amber in the doorway. "Come on in, if you can stand to. Right now, my father is complaining about the beeping of his machines around him. You'd think the world was coming to an end."

"How are you doing, Mr. Beaumont?" she asked Luke's father.

"What? You don't call me Big Dan anymore?" Luke's father asked.

Amber shook her head. "You don't look all that big anymore, Mr. Beaumont. You need more muscles."

She was joking, but Big Dan made a lot of noise turning in the bed to face the wall. He was curled up like a boiled shrimp.

Luke knew why he was acting like a five-year-old. This was the hospital that Valerie Lynn had died in, and she'd been transported to the cemetery in probably that very hearse.

But that didn't mean Big Dan had to act like a juvenile delinquent.

Luke was about to tell him to behave himself when Nurse Margie Proctor stormed into the room. She was a little younger than Big Dan and had lost her husband around the same time he had lost his wife.

She lunged to his bedside, hands on her hips. "What are you doing disrupting my floor, Daniel Beaumont? This is a hospital, and we have lots of people with very serious illnesses. They don't want to hear you whining. Now button it!"

He turned into a regular person right before their eyes. "I'm not disrupting anything. Just give me some pills and let me go, will you, Margie?"

Margie used to be a frequent visitor to the Beaumont Ranch because she'd been in a book club with Valerie Lynn. Luke remembered Margie as a no-nonsense nurse, but quick with a laugh and a smile. In fact, Margie had tended his mother and was there to pick up the pieces when she died.

"The doctor on call will be right in, and we don't just hand out pills like candy." She plumped his pillow, smoothed his sheets and had him eating out of her hand.

His father looked…smitten.

Could that be?

Maybe. Margie had honey-chestnut hair, twinkly brown eyes and a perfect shape. But more than that, Margie was nice.

There was that word again.

Luke went over to Amber who was sitting on an extra chair and reading messages on her cell phone.

"I think my father's going to be okay," Luke said.

"You do?"

"Yeah. Look at him over there, flirting with Margie."

Amber giggled. "I know. I've been watching them out of the corner of my eye."

They both laughed and Luke added, "Looks to me like she likes him, until she finds out he's in alcohol rehab, that is."

Amber grinned. "Oh, she probably knows. Small town. And he arrived here in a hearse. It's something that people will be talking about for years to come."

"True."

He stood and paced a bit to stretch his legs. He'd talk to his father, but he was still occupied with Margie.

"If I wasn't so cash poor, I'd buy the town a new ambulance," he said.

"Don't stop there. Our fleet of exactly four cop cars is ancient, and so is the fire truck. We could use two fire trucks and two ambulances if you're going to get your checkbook out."

"Wish I could fund them. I really do."

"Hey, uh…wait a minute!" Amber said. "A rodeo! We could have a rodeo in your outdoor arena. And you have bleachers. We could rent more bleachers and put them around the ring. Cars and RVs could park in the south pasture, and the refreshments alone could bring in a ton of money, but the real attraction would be all the bull riding stars, who are your friends. Your brothers are an attraction, too."

"Amber, are you talking about what I think you are?"

"A fund-raiser. First, I thought of just bull riding, but there's such talent in Beaumont, we should throw an amateur rodeo and use all your new stock, but have a professional bull riding section with some of your pals."

She was so excited, her face was flushed. Her green eyes were twinkling and she looked…animated and… beautiful. When he'd noticed her in high school, it had crossed his mind that she was fairly pretty, but now she was gorgeous. And she was just as beautiful inside as she was outside. Some women weren't, like Lucy McClennan.

Lucy was hot. He'd dated her just after the senior prom through the summer before he joined the PBR. Lucy turned heads wherever she went. She was arm candy, and that's all she was. She had a mean streak in her a mile wide, and her jealousy knew no bounds.

Luke couldn't handle a jealous woman, especially when he was meeting and greeting his fans. That was when her claws really came out. No, thanks.

"What do you think, Luke?"

"Huh? Oh yeah, the fund-raiser."

He was about to tell her that her idea was brilliant when Margie walked over to them.

"Here comes Dr. Paulson now," Margie said. "Would you two leave the room for a while? Then later he will come and speak to you. There's a nice waiting room just down the hall on the right."

"Sure, Margie."

It seemed natural for him to put his hand on her back and walk with her down the hallway to the waiting room.

They sank into a black faux-leather couch that should have been scrapped years ago.

"Your idea for a fund-raiser is a good one," Luke said. "But we'd have to hold it in August, before I have to leave. That's only two months away. Can we pull it off?"

"You've never seen me in action," Amber said. "I'll do it for the town. Then I'm going to leave, too. I got an offer."

Luke was shocked. He'd never really thought that she'd leave Beaumont. "Seriously, you're going to leave? Where?"

Amber smiled. "To Spirit Springs, Oklahoma. It's northeast of here. I've accepted a provisional appointment with the Oklahoma State Police. I start after Labor Day."

Chapter Twelve

When Amber told Luke about accepting a provisional appointment with the Oklahoma State Police, there didn't seem to be any excitement in her heart.

Wasn't that the job she'd wanted forever?

There was almost a feeling of dread.

"A provisional appointment, huh?" he asked.

"They got some special waivers and are allowed to hire current law enforcement personnel, but it means that I'll have to take the test for the position when it's offered and be reachable on the civil service list. Then I'll have to pass an agility test and whatever else. Oh, and then there's their famous investigation of me and my family. Which I hope they pass."

"Will they be an obstacle?" he asked.

"If you were the Superintendent of State Police, would you hold my family's…uh…past illegal activities against me?"

"Nope. Not at all."

"Wouldn't you think that if I was in law enforcement and they were doing something illegal, I should turn them in?"

He rubbed his chin. "That's a tough one. They're your

family. If they are doing harm to others, yes. That's an easy one."

"Moonshining could do harm to others. Especially if their customers drive drunk and hurt someone," Amber reminded him.

"Yeah. I see your dilemma. I also saw boxes and boxes of canning jars stacked six deep against the wall of your dad's dining room."

"I saw them, too. But I checked. They were empty. But just looking at them made my stomach turn."

He shrugged. "I haven't heard anything about your family making shine. Believe me. All my workers would be talking about it."

She let out a deep breath. "Good to know. Thanks."

"Wouldn't the state police investigators be concerned with you living with a son of a man you arrested three times?"

Oh, no! It had never even dawned on her that giving Luke a place to stay would jeopardize her state police appointment.

Before she could formulate an answer, Nurse Margie stuck her head into the room. "You can come and visit now, but don't stay long. Dan is pretty tired and he's going to be busy tomorrow with tests."

"Thanks, Margie," Luke said. "If he's cranky with you, let me know, and I'll have a man-to-man with him."

"Your father has been a perfect gentleman," Margie said. "And very cooperative."

"No kidding?" Amber asked. "He's miserable with me. He either gives me the stink-eye or pretends that I'm not in the room."

"No kidding?" Margie echoed. "Excuse me. I have other patients to check."

"Thanks, Margie," Luke said to the departing nurse. Then he turned to Amber.

"You know…you did arrest Big Dan three times." Luke raised an eyebrow. "He told me that you were stalking him."

"Serious?"

He nodded.

"Do you believe him?" she asked.

"Nah."

"Are you just saying that because you need a place to stay?" Amber asked.

"No. I'm not. But three times?"

"As you know, but I'll tell you again, he busted up the bar three times. They called to complain three times, and I took action three times. Each time, it got a little more serious because he didn't get it, Luke. He just didn't get it. Haven't we gone over this a couple of times? What aren't you saying?"

"That maybe you didn't look too hard at your father and brothers recently because they might be guilty of cattle rustling and that might ruin your potential new job."

"Oh, so that's what's got you thinking? You think I'm ignoring what my family might be doing because it'll look bad for me when the time comes?" she asked. "And by the way, I looked at the jars they had in the house and they were empty."

"You just spot-checked the top row and just assumed they were all empty. True?"

That was true, but how did he know?

Oh, darn it. Luke was probably right. She just didn't want to believe that her father and brothers were up to no good. She stopped walking and bit back angry tears. "Look, you don't need me to accompany you to see your father. You go ahead. I'll wait in the car. And then maybe we can drive to a car parts store and get you a battery for your truck. And how about calling around to hotels? Maybe they have some vacancies by now."

"I'm sorry if I hit a sore spot."

"Here's your father's room. Give him my best, won't you?" She turned and left him standing there. "I'll give you fifteen minutes, then you can call a taxi."

"Okay."

She left as fast as she could without disturbing the patients and nurses in the hallways. She had to get away from Luke before she said something she'd regret. But, oh, she got her message, though.

But so had he.

Finally she was in the lobby and out the door. She unlocked her car and slid into the driver's seat.

She punched the steering wheel. That hurt.

Amber felt unhinged, off-centered.

She'd just basically told Luke to get out of her car and get out of her apartment.

She was going to miss him. She'd cared for him forever. They'd kissed, for heaven's sake. They'd *really* kissed.

Was there some truth in what Luke said?

No. Impossible.

WHAT THE HELL *just happened?*

He'd just made a simple suggestion that Amber might be a little—what was the word?—biased. As far as her family was concerned, maybe she didn't want to face the truth.

He wanted to ask his father to give Amber a break and not hold his arrests against her because she was only doing her job, but Big Dan was fighting sleep and he didn't want to stress him out by having a fight.

"Close your eyes, Dad. I'm leaving."

"You still fixing up the ranch?"

"You know I am. I have two crews working on it and some other paid help. Others have refused pay…like Amber, Slim Gomez and a bunch of others."

"Humph! Where's all this money coming from?"

"From Reed, Jesse and me, and from a historical grant that's been in the works for months," Luke said.

"Historical grant? Better the taxpayers should save their money."

"Let's not hash this out anymore. Get some sleep. I'm going to say goodbye now."

"Then say it and go!"

"Great to see you, too, Dad."

"Humph."

Luke left the room and checked his watch. The clock was ticking to catch a ride from Amber.

Just his luck; the elevators were shut off and getting mopped. He hit the stairs, prepared to go down eight floors.

He didn't know why, but stairs always made him dizzy.

Hurrying down, he had to pause on the landing and stop his head from spinning. He was only on the fourth floor.

He had to catch his breath again in the lobby. He checked his watch. Twenty minutes had gone by and Amber had only given him fifteen.

Oh, for heaven's sake, she'd wait an extra five minutes, wouldn't she?

He checked the parking lot and, in particular, the space where she'd parked.

Her car was gone.

Dammit! She wasn't kidding.

He went back into the lobby, where the numbers of the two taxi firms in Beaumont were posted. He called the first one. Fred's Cab.

Fred's wife Mavis said that he was attending a culinary class at the community college. "Do you think he wants to drive a cab for the rest of his life?"

"Uh…maybe not, Mavis, but his number was posted in the hospital lobby."

"I'll take care of scratching that out. Call Evan Volney. He loves the business."

"Thanks, Mavis."

He punched in the number for Evan Volney. Evan was nearby and would be at the front of the hospital "in a sec."

Luke paced the sidewalk outside. He found a shadowy spot and decided to burn off some nervous energy. He did some yoga stretches, which he swore helped his riding, and did a hundred pushups. Then he ran in place until Evan arrived.

"I don't know the exact address, but it's over the Happy Tea Pot or something like that," Luke said.

"Sergeant Amber Chapman's place?"

"You know it?" Luke asked.

"Sure. We had a couple of dates, but she's too cop-ish. She noticed that my registration was expired and so was my license. She told me that if I put another person in my cab before I took care of both items, she was going to arrest me." He chuckled. "Real romantic, huh?"

"That sounds like her." Luke chuckled and sat back in the seat, satisfied that Amber would be great in her new state police job.

"Hey, Evan. What's the hotel situation now? Are they still packed?"

"Still packed. Now there's graduation at Beaumont Community College and OSU."

"Maybe I can sleep in my barn," Luke muttered. "Or put up my tent."

Just as he said that, the skies opened up and it started raining. Pouring.

Evan pulled in at the back of the Happy Tea Pot and Luke paid him and gave him a nice tip. Then he took a deep breath and climbed the stairs to Amber's apartment, not knowing what to expect.

BY THE TIME Amber got to the door and opened it, Luke was soaked.

"Amber, I came to pick up my stuff and then I'll get out of your hair."

"Where are you going?" she asked. "Not that it's any of my business."

"Don't know yet, but would you mind if I get my gear? It's in your spare bedroom."

Amber nodded. "Of course. Go ahead."

She'd been tempted to toss his stuff out the door and onto the lawn, but she'd answered enough domestic calls to realize that the stunt was too juvenile.

She'd brought Luke Beaumont here; she should give him a place to stay, no matter how mad she was at him. He'd said something like that before, about her being biased, and she'd even questioned herself, but this time, it had just gotten to her.

The man had gotten to her, and normally she wouldn't give a hoot, but she cared for Luke and his opinion.

Luke came out of the bedroom just as she was making herself a meatloaf sandwich with lettuce and mayo. He looked at it as if it was prime rib.

"Luke, before you start drooling, would you like a sandwich?"

"To go?"

"You can eat it here." Amber put it on a plate and added a dill pickle.

"I've been dreaming of this meatloaf," he said, taking a big bite then walking over to the kitchen table and taking a seat.

He watched as Amber made another sandwich and realized he was eating what Amber had made for herself.

Amber was a thoughtful and caring woman, and he should shut up about her family. He wouldn't hurt her for the world, but he should really pay attention to what he was saying.

"Amber, I apologize. I shouldn't have said what I did. Let's call a truce. I really want to work with you on my cattle rustling tomorrow. Remember I was going to loan you a horse and we were going to go out in the morning and check tracks? But then there was the Bull Riders' Ball and then my dad's heart attack, and, well, we haven't made much progress on the investigation."

She was silent, as if she was weighing the pros and cons of accepting his apology. He waited, shifting on his feet, hoping that they'd be back to where they were before he opened his big mouth.

"Okay, Luke. We're good. And I'm all for a truce. Stay here, because I know there's no other place for you to stay in town. I made some calls and found out that there are still no rooms. And, yes, I need a horse, so I suppose I have to let you come with me."

Luke let out a deep breath. "Good, it's settled, then. Status quo. Thanks for the place to stay."

"Quit thanking me and all that… You're just so…"

"Nice?" he supplied.

"Uh-huh."

Luke snapped his fingers. "Do you mind if we go bright and early in the morning to the Auto Palace? I'll get the battery for my pickup. I can put it in. This will be the last trip lugging me around."

"Good. Then you'll have your own wheels."

"About time, huh?"

She shrugged. "About time." If truth be told, she liked the company.

"I have to go to work now, so see you later. Lock up, okay?"

"Okay."

THE NEXT MORNING they had plans to hit the road for the Auto Palace for Luke's battery.

Luke was sleeping on the couch, shirt off, one arm over his head, one at his side. When she wasn't looking at his muscled riding arms, she was staring at his chest.

Finally, after tearing herself away, she made herself a cup of jasmine tea.

As soon as she could find the time, she really should check *all* those boxes at her father's place. Just to ease her own mind and to prove to Luke that her father was innocent.

Not that she had to prove anything to Luke. He had his own problems with Big Dan's issues.

She just didn't feel the same toward Luke since their altercation over their fathers and which one was the most trouble.

Sheesh. It was like they were in grammar school.

They were both more mature than that.

She was going to forget about it and concentrate on who was rustling Luke's cattle. When she solved the case, she'd leave Beaumont County. It would probably be the last important case of her career here.

And she couldn't wait to get started at the Beaumont Ranch and solve the rustling case.

Chapter Thirteen

Luke leaned on the weather-damaged wood that circled the corral and looked over the horses in his remuda. He picked out two.

"Amber, I haven't had a chance to ride these myself, but Slim Gomez swears that they are perfect saddle horses."

"I can ride. Don't worry about me."

Luke shook his head. "It might be hopeless to find tracks. We've had nothing but rain for the past couple of days. A lot of rain."

"I know, but maybe we can find something."

"Let's go, then. Slim said he'd saddle them up for us."

They walked into the barn and found two quarter horses saddled and ready to go. They were both stunning—a chestnut with a shiny brown coat with red highlights, and one with a mottled gray coat.

Amber was floating on air. It'd been a long time since she'd been riding and now she was getting the best of the best.

Judging by the grin on Luke's face, he was thinking the same thing she was.

"It seems like forever since I've been on a horse."

"And these are beauties. Do you know their names?" Amber asked.

Luke petted the taller of the two mares. "I haven't gotten around to finding that out yet, but I will."

He got on his horse. "I think I'll call her Chestnut for the time being. It's obvious, but I like the name. How about yours?"

"Irma," Amber said. "After my first boss when I worked in the steno pool of a law firm." Two hops and she made it on top of Irma.

"Your horse reminds you of Irma?"

"She has Irma's grayish hair color."

Luke laughed. "Where would you like to begin?"

"Can you find a trail to the northeast pasture?" she asked.

"My memory might be foggy, but I think I can."

All the pounding of the hammers was making Chestnut and Irma nervous.

"Let's get out of here. Then we can stop and talk."

Luke took off at a trot and Amber tried to keep pace with him. He was born in the saddle; she'd infrequently ridden the horses of various friends.

Amber had begged her parents for a horse when she was young. When that hadn't worked, she'd prayed to God and Santa Claus every Christmas for a horse. Then when her mother left, she'd asked her father again, but he'd said he didn't have room for a horse. He needed the room for his junk car parts.

That was when she'd really started to hate the junkyard. Up until then, it was just something the kids in school teased her about. She'd hated the teasing, but her mother told her that someday she'd go to college and be away from the rusting mess.

She and her mom had both gotten out of the junk-yard. Amber went to college, and her mother worked in the college's main cafeteria. They were roommates at a nearby apartment, and it was the best time of Amber's life. She'd gotten to know her more, and they talked like mothers and daughters should. Above all, she realized how much her mother loved her father.

Both of them still hated the junkyard because it was a blight on the pretty town of Beaumont, and because it surrounded the once pretty little bungalow where Amber and her brothers grew up.

Luke slowed Chestnut to a walk and Amber listened to the creaking of the leather saddle. She hadn't heard that in a long time, and she'd missed it. It was a small thing that only she identified with, but it reminded her of an earlier time in her life.

Now her sounds were the rasp of handcuffs, the howl of sirens and the metallic banging of cell doors.

"A penny for your thoughts, Amber."

"There're not worth that much."

"Tell me anyway."

"I was just thinking about how I wanted a horse when I was younger. I mean, who didn't want one when they were a kid? Every day, I saw yours grazing in the pasture and I used to pretend that they were mine. I was partial to palominos or pure white ones, or the black ones with white socks." She laughed. "I wanted them all, and you had them all. You and your brothers were the luckiest kids on earth."

"I know. I know. We had a great childhood. The whole ranch was our playground."

"Who are you kidding? The whole town of Beaumont was your playground!"

"I know…and we were incorrigible."

She tried for a stern expression. "You sure were, but that was a long time ago. Now you, Jesse and Reed are all big-shot, professional bull riders."

"Who would have thought?"

She smiled. "I did. I remember how good you were on the high school rodeo team."

"You came to the events to watch me?"

"Yes—I mean no. I mean, I came to watch everyone. Not just you."

Her face had to be flaming. He'd caught her off guard.

She had gone to see everyone ride, but it was Luke that made her heart race every time he rode. And she'd held her breath when he'd slid onto the back of his bull and didn't let it out until he was safe.

Amber still did that, even while watching Luke ride on TV.

They rode side by side across a field. The wind kicked up, making the wheat sway to its own rhythm, but at least it wasn't raining again.

She changed the subject. "The swaying wheat is hypnotizing." She yawned. "I don't think I got enough sleep last night."

"Were you thinking of our fight?"

"It's probably for the best that we don't discuss it anymore," Amber said.

"That has my vote." Luke leaned forward in the saddle and looked down the narrow dirt road. "But we should discuss it, Amber. I don't want anything hanging between us, so you go first."

"I figure that in order to steal ten cattle, he—or they—would have had a truck. Like a stock transport. It's pretty flat here, but with the extra weight of the stock, the tracks might be somewhat intact."

"Just what I've been thinking," he said. "Better yet, the wheat might be crushed. That would show the route the truck would have taken."

They walked their horses and Amber scanned the area for some kind of clues.

"What's that?" she asked. "Over there. On that bush. That black cloth." Amber pointed. "It looks familiar. If I'm not mistaken, it has little American flags on it. Right?"

Luke walked over to the object and was about to dislodge it from the bush when Amber yelled, "Don't touch it. I have gloves. I'll do it."

"Little American flags are on it."

The look on his face had Amber realizing that he'd seen it before, too.

"It's a bandanna," he said. "The kind the bikers wear around here. The Beaumont Bombers."

Then it hit her and her stomach started to churn. "No way. It can't be. Must be a mistake."

"Sorry, Amber, but we both saw your brother Ronnie wearing it when we had barbecue at your dad's house. Then again when he came to work on my pickup and yet again when he helped on the ranch house."

"Like you said, it's common to the Beaumont Bombers. It could be anyone's."

Amber hurried over to the evidence, plucked it carefully off the bush, and put it in a glassine bag. Then the unmistakable scent of musk that was Ronnie's aftershave drifted from it.

"Luke, this hasn't been here long. Certainly not in the rain we've been having. It's not even damp."

"Is it Ronnie's?" Luke asked.

"I'll ask him."

Her stomach sank, and suddenly she couldn't breathe. She knew very well that the bandanna belonged to her brother. Luke had better not make any remarks about the Chapmans because her last nerve was jumping. He nodded, then pointed. "And look at the truck tracks that lead away from here. They go right toward your father's junkyard then disappear onto the highway."

She could see the tracks very clearly because the wheat and tall grasses were tamped down.

"Circumstantial evidence," she said.

Luke shrugged. "Maybe. Maybe not."

"What do you mean by that?" she said slowly. Her face heated with anger, and her mouth was so dry that she would give her right arm for a glass of water. "You already have Ronnie convicted and hung from the nearest cottonwood as a rustler. Well, Luke, this isn't the Wild West, and I haven't seen a cottonwood tree around here."

He grinned. "We have others that'll do."

Amber took pictures with her cell phone and the department-issued camera. "Let's go."

"Yeah. I want to check on my father. How about waiting for me to talk to Ronnie?"

"I'll talk to Ronnie on my own time. You are not going to be present. I'll talk to Ronnie and rule him out."

"Or you might consider him a suspect."

"Not my brother. He wouldn't do such a thing," Amber snapped.

"You have three brothers. Maybe Ronnie had help."

"No!"

"That's why I want to be with you," Luke said. "You

aren't keeping an open mind. Or maybe you need to speak with Captain Fitz and run things by him."

She began to fume. "Not necessary. And let me remind you that I'm the detective, not you."

"Okay. I'll back off and let you handle it, but let me be with you when you speak with Ronnie, or I'll just take him out for a couple of beers and…"

"I'm asking you one more time, Luke. Let me handle this or I'll charge you with obstructing justice."

They walked the horses the rest of the way in silence. When they came to an open field, Luke mounted and trotted Chestnut, then galloped.

He wants to get away from me, as much as I want to get away from him.

She arrived at the makeshift barn after him.

"You don't have to groom and put away tack," Luke said. "Slim will take care of finding someone to brush them. I have to get to the hospital, and I'm sure you have investigating to do."

They tied the horses and Slim appeared. "I'll take care of them. Go ahead."

"Thanks, Slim," they both said.

Amber couldn't wait to get away from Luke and, obviously, the feeling was mutual.

Luke rubbed his chin. "Things have changed between us since we found Ronnie's bandanna, haven't they?"

"I don't know for certain that it's his."

"There's Ronnie over there." Luke pointed to a pile of lumber at the side of the old barn. Ronnie was picking through it as if looking for a particular piece.

"I'll go talk to him," she said. "You go and check on Big Dan."

But Luke was already headed in Ronnie's direction, and he didn't wait before he started questioning him.

"Ronnie, where's your black bandanna with the American flags on it?" Luke asked.

Amber put her hands on her hips. "You don't have to answer his question, Ronnie. I'm the one investigating the rustling. He just loaned me a horse this morning."

Ronnie stood up to his full six-foot-four frame. He looked down at Luke, then at Amber.

"What are you two blabbing about?" Ronnie asked.

"Where's your bandanna with the flags on it?" Luke asked again.

Amber sighed. "You might as well answer that, Ronnie."

"I lost it somewhere," Ronnie said. "Why do you ask?"

"When's the last time you had it?" Amber asked.

Ronnie shifted from leg to leg. "I don't know. Again, why are you asking?"

"I'll tell you later." Amber pulled out the evidence bag with the cloth in it. "Is this yours?"

"Looks like mine," Ronnie said. "Let me see it, and I'll tell you for sure."

She handed the bag to her brother and made eye contact with Luke. She thought he looked way too smug and arrogant.

She'd show Luke. *Ronnie will say that it isn't his.*

"Yeah, that's mine," Ronnie stated. "It's my favorite. All the Beaumont Bombers wear that one. Thanks for finding it."

"How do you know it's not another Beaumont Bomber who is missing theirs?" Amber asked, hoping for a good answer.

Ronnie shrugged. "I don't. All I know is that this one is mine."

"Then how did it get up on the hill behind the junk-yard, brother?"

He shrugged. "Damned if I know, sis."

"And there were tracks, like truck tracks, leading from where your bandanna was, past the junkyard to the high-way."

"O-*kay*," Ronnie said, drawing out the word. "Why are you telling me this?" His eyes grew as wide as Luke's belt buckle. "You don't think that I had anything to do with rustling Luke's cattle, do you?"

Amber remained silent and was glad that Luke re-mained silent, too, and didn't butt in.

Amber sighed. "Of course I don't think that you had anything to do with the rustling, but I have to check it out. Ronnie, think hard—when was the last time you saw the thing?"

"It was hotter than hell while I was working on the barn roof." He paused to think. "I was having lunch. I took it off, poured water on it and wiped my face. Then I put it on a tree branch to dry next to the barn. I guess I forgot to get it when I left that day."

"Someone else could have easily taken it." Amber turned to Luke. "And planted it up there on the hill to throw suspicion onto Ronnie."

Ronnie swore under his breath. "Who would hate me that freakin' much?" He turned to Luke. "Dude, you gotta believe that I'd never take your cattle."

Luke shrugged. "The investigation has just started. Trust Amber—or should I say, Sergeant Chapman. She'll get to the bottom of the whole mess."

Amber had to turn away before she laughed out loud.

Luke was telling Ronnie to trust her, when clearly Luke didn't trust her himself.

Her life certainly was interesting.

She had to take Ronnie's statement at headquarters. Wasn't her brother going to be thrilled when she dragged him down there? *Not!*

"Ronnie, any idea who made those tracks?" she asked.

"How would I know, sis? I didn't even notice them when I left home to come here to help. And I'm starting to think that helping out isn't such a great idea."

"Don't think that," Amber said. "Like Luke told you, I'll get to the bottom of this. Don't worry, but I do need you to come down to the department to give a statement."

"Now?"

"No. When you're done," she said. "I'll be there until eleven o'clock tonight."

"You know I avoid that place like it carries the plague," Ronnie said.

"We don't have a plague going at the present time. You're safe." Amber smiled. "I think I'll be the only one there along with the dispatcher."

"You're not going to arrest me, are you, Amber?"

"I'll arrest you if you don't show. Shall we say eight o'clock?"

Chapter Fourteen

Ronnie did show at eight o'clock, right on time.

"Let's get going, Sergeant Sis. I have a date with your dispatcher." He waved at her through the window and she waved back.

"Emily Johnson hasn't gone out with anyone since her husband died two years ago. How did you do it?"

"With my Chapman charm," Ronnie said.

"Uh-huh." She found the affidavit file on her computer and tried to get her brother to focus, but he was more concerned about where to take Emily.

"There's going to be nothing open at midnight, Ronnie, except the bowling alley. At least they have pizza. You'd better order one ahead of time."

"Great idea, sis." Ronnie pulled out his cell phone.

"Not now! We have to get this over with. Then you can play on your cell phone."

He gave her an exaggerated salute.

She breezed through the affidavit and the door to the department opened.

Luke Beaumont!

Her heart was going to jump right out of her body and her cheeks heated. Every time she saw Luke, it was the same reaction and didn't lessen in intensity.

Instead it increased.

She couldn't help but sigh. She wasn't in the mood to fight with him or to have him tell her how to run her investigation.

But he didn't look happy. Matter of fact, Luke's facial expressions morphed from sadness to being mad enough to chew glass.

"Hi, Ronnie. Hi, Amber," he said, barely moving his lips.

Ronnie held up his hand for a high-five and Luke pretty much ignored him. Then it looked like he'd decided that he'd better slap Ronnie's hand, and did so—sort of.

Something was terribly wrong.

"Hey, Luke. I just finished officially telling my story. Who would have thought that a simple bandanna would cause so much attention?"

"Not me," Luke said. "But I have something to tell Amber. I mean, Sergeant Chapman."

Amber braced herself for what might be coming.

"I found this near the tracks that the truck left. I was looking around, and found this thing." He pulled out a plastic bag and inside was a red pocketknife.

"That looks like Kyle's," Ronnie said. "Where did you find it?"

"It was just outside the eighteen-wheeler tracks that led from my northeast pasture on the side of your father's junkyard. It was in the tall grass. So, you think it's your brother Kyle's?"

"I know so," Ronnie said. "He got it for Christmas from my father when we were kids. It was like the best gift of his life, and he's never without the thing. He scratched his name on it. You could probably see it if you held it up to the light. He was wondering where his knife went."

"I'll get him down here for a statement," Amber said, picking up the phone to call her brother.

"Any other Chapman litter on the scene of the crime?" Ronnie asked. "Doesn't it seem funny that our stuff is scattered all over?"

"Or else you both stole Beaumont cattle," Luke snapped. Ronnie got up from his chair and stood toe-to-toe with Luke.

Amber picked up her phone, contacted Kyle and issued orders to Luke and Ronnie in between her conversation.

"Whoever throws the first punch goes to jail, and I mean it." She pulled her handcuffs from the pouch on her utility belt. "Keep your hands at your sides. And each of you take four steps back. Now!"

They did. She didn't know who would win in a fist fight, but Ronnie was tall and powerful. Luke was shorter, but had cannons for arms.

She'd hate to see them fighting and she didn't want either one of them hurt.

She hung up the phone.

"Kyle told me he realized he'd lost his pocketknife around the same time Ronnie lost his bandanna. Kyle was using it to slice up an apple that he brought for lunch. He said that he put it in his jacket pocket and hung his jacket up on a nail on the side of the barn."

"Someone could have easily lifted the knife from the pocket," Luke said.

Ronnie grunted. "Duh."

Amber put her hands on her hips. "Okay, Ronnie, you're free to go. Wait for Emily someplace else."

Ronnie held his hand out for Luke to shake. "Dude,

I really hope you find the rustlers. I do. But they ain't the Chapmans."

Luke took his hand and they shook. "I hope not, Ronnie. I really do."

Ronnie left and Luke took the seat he vacated, next to Amber's desk. "Got a minute, Amber?"

"Yes. Yes, of course." She hit a button on her computer and her screen reverted to the logo of the Beaumont County Sheriff's Department. "What's up?"

"My father needs a couple of stents in his chest. Then he'll be okay. That's going to happen tomorrow at ten in the morning. The doctor told me that he was lucky the EMTs were there to stabilize him and that Donny Cushman was available with his hearse."

"I'm glad that the medical staff got to the root of your dad's problems, Luke, and I know the hearse bothers everyone." Amber nodded. "I really do plan on working on the rodeo to raise money for a new ambulance. In fact, I'll volunteer my whole family...you know, the people you think are cattle rustlers. That family."

Luke tapped his finger on Amber's desk. "I hope that the rustlers are found soon. Dammit, I hate to think that anyone in your family was involved, but I guess I can't help myself."

"The Chapmans have always been the first that people think of when trouble is concerned. Usually, they did it, but not this time, Luke. It's too staged. Too set up. I'd bet my badge on the fact that the Chapmans aren't involved."

"No need to do that."

"That's one of the reasons why I became a cop. To show the good people of Beaumont that a Chapman can be on the right side of the law."

"Aw... Amber. It's just that their moonshining affected

a lot of people. Particularly high-schoolers, like your senior prom date, Crazy Kenny Fowler."

"Why did you have to remind me of that night?" She
shook her head. "Crazy Kenny Fowler."

"Did you know that I walked you home that night?"
Luke said. "I was worried about you."

"You *what*?"

"I walked you home. I stayed in the shadows, so you
wouldn't see me. I didn't want you embarrassed any more
than you already were because you were crying. You
took your shoes off and walked home in stocking feet.
Funny, I don't remember the name of my prom date, but
I remember walking you home that evening."

She felt like crying now. "Luke, I didn't know. I appreciate that you did that. It's so sweet of you. It seems like a
lifetime ago, but then again, it feels like it was yesterday."

"Next time there's a senior prom, we'll go."

"Are you on crack?"

"We'll go as chaperones."

She laughed. "I accept." Amber made another vow to
go to Marco's Fit-nasium.

"Luke, not to change the subject, but I do have a brilliant idea. Someone is framing my family, so I want to
lay a trap."

"I'm listening."

"My only brother who hasn't…uh…*lost* something is
Aaron. So, when Aaron works at your place tomorrow,
I think he should somehow leave something behind. I'm
thinking of his Oklahoma Sooners baseball cap. He's
never without it, and he has his name inside it. Since his
years at Boy Scout camp, he's put his name on everything he owns."

"Great idea. I can keep one eye peeled for his baseball

cap. Maybe I can see who takes it. How about if Aaron loses his cap when I'm there to watch? I have to head to the hospital before my father's surgery. After, I can drive to my ranch. Then I'll go back up to the hospital for when he wakes up. After I see him, I can hit my ranch again."

"Don't worry, Luke. I'll be there to observe. You just take care of Big Dan."

"Call me when you have news."

"I will," Amber said. "But maybe nothing will happen."

"Maybe something will." He paused and looked out the window. "Just in case you're thinking of working at the ranch, don't do it. You've done enough for me."

"I'll be working, Luke. I'll be working on your investigation."

"How about a snack for when you come home?"

She winked. "Will you be cooking?"

"I'll be buying it from the sub shop. What would you like?"

"The Beaumont Beefer with the works and their special sauce. No anchovies."

"Sounds good. I'll make it two."

Amber grinned. "Your life will never be the same."

"My life hasn't been the same since you showed up in my line at the autographing."

Amber wanted to tell Luke that she hadn't been the same since she'd first noticed him, circa fourth grade.

Now she had something to look forward to after work, and that was dinner with Luke.

First, she had to take Kyle's statement. Then she had to call Aaron and explain her plan, and let him know that he'd have to do without his lucky Sooner hat, if only for a while if all went right.

Her immediate concern was to get Luke out the door before Kyle showed up. She didn't want the same exchange between Luke and Kyle as the one between Luke and Ronnie.

Amber didn't want to get him out the door. She could talk to him about the bull riding fund-raiser. Or they could talk about nothing. Even if they didn't talk, she liked just being with him.

Luke stood. "I'll head out now and I'll pick up some beer and wine and soda. Do we need anything else?"

"Thick-sliced bacon."

"Oh, baby, you're singing my song! How about some pancake mix?" he asked.

"I make my pancakes from scratch."

"No kidding! I'd better get to the gym. Your cooking is just too good. I'll never be able to bend to ride my bulls, and I'll have to ride naked because my jeans will never fit me."

She pictured him naked, not on a bull, but lying in bed, waiting for her. She'd be in the bathroom slipping into something sexy—her black-and-red lace nightgown—and when she came out...

She'd bought the sexy nightgown for, um, uh... what's-his-name, but never put it on. She'd decided he wasn't good enough for such a gown.

Luke Beaumont was.

"Luke, I'll walk you out. I need some fresh air."

That wasn't all she needed.

SHE TOOK KYLE'S statement at the office.

It was quick and to the point. He had been washing his hands with the hose and slipped his pocketknife into the pocket of his jean jacket. Then he'd hung it over a nail and had lunch. He hadn't needed the jacket because it was warm while he was working, so at the end of the day he'd grabbed it off the hook and only noticed that his knife was missing when he hung it up at home.

Then she spoke with Aaron at her father's house.

Aaron was on board, though Amber had to swear that she'd replace his Sooner hat if anything happened to it.

She also had to calm him down. If he caught someone stealing his hat, she told him that he couldn't do anything. Nothing at all.

That didn't sit well with Aaron.

While she was there, she checked every box of bottles lined up against the wall. They were all empty. *Good for them.*

Though she wondered where the filled jars were.

She remembered that while she'd been directing traffic at the courthouse, her father had come back from getting his license. He had sworn to her that he wasn't moonshining, but she still just couldn't bring herself to believe him.

Maybe she should follow him.

Follow her own father? What was she thinking?

She didn't want to find trouble. She already had enough history for the state police to reject her for a permanent assignment.

She drove to her apartment and changed out of her uniform, read the paper and went over her notes on the case.

When Luke arrived with their sub sandwiches, he uncorked some wine and she got out the glasses.

Mmm...chardonnay. How did he know that she liked chard?

"A toast." Luke held up his glass. "To you, Amber. Thanks for letting me stay here. Thanks for working on catching the rustlers, and thanks for getting help for my father."

She raised her glass and took a drink, then toasted him. "To Luke Beaumont, for coming back to town and fixing up our finest landmark and tourist attraction."

He laughed and drained his glass. He seemed more like a beer guy and was probably only drinking wine for her.

"Luke, let's switch channels and talk about the bull riding fund-raiser. I noticed that the stands and the arena had some destruction."

"I'm already on it. Just as soon as the barn and the paddock are done, I'll move the men to the arena. Some of the chairs need to be screwed down again. Some of the bleachers need to be replaced and painted. It'll be done before Labor Day."

Amber's heart sank. "But then work on your house will be delayed."

"I have a crew working on that, too. I said I'd do the fund-raiser for an ambulance, and that's what I'm going to do. I don't want anyone going to the hospital in a hearse anymore. It's a bad omen!"

Amber looked at her notebook. "I'm going to get posters made up and announce it in the local paper. It's been a long time since the Beaumont Ranch had its famous annual rodeo. You can expect a fabulous turnout."

"You'll take care of traffic control and parking?" Luke asked.

"The Beaumont County Sheriff's Department will direct traffic. Seniors at the high school will handle the parking."

"Great. What else?" Luke asked.

"Barbecue. Can't have a rodeo without barbecue," she said.

"Smokin' Sammy's House of Hickory. They can take care of catering."

"Great idea," Amber said.

"Portable toilets. Get a bunch of them and spare no expense."

She laughed. "I wrote that down already."

"You're way ahead of me. What else?" he asked.

"You need to contact your brothers and your bull riding pals and get them on board. I'll put their names on the posters and on the press release."

"They'll love it. They're all publicity hogs."

"T-shirts. People love tees." Amber wrote furiously in her notebook.

"That one's easy." Luke winked. "I'll contact the PBR and ask them to send some people to run a merchandise booth, and they'll bring items to sell."

"Done."

"We're going to need an announcer," Amber said.

Luke snapped his fingers. "That's easy. I'll do it."

Amber smiled. "I was hoping that you'd say that."

"You were?"

"Yes. You'll be perfect." Amber nodded.

"Perfect? You think I'm perfect?" He winked.

"As an arena announcer."

"But I'm perfect?" he asked, eyebrows raised.

"Luke, I've never learned how to flirt with a man. What you see is what you get. I'm a cop. If you're expecting cute banter from me, I just can't do it."

Luke stood and offered Amber his hand. "You're a woman first. You're a cop second."

She took his hand. "What are you doing, Luke?"

He moved closer and took her in his arms and swayed.

He was humming something, but she couldn't quite identify the tune.

They swayed and he led her around her kitchen and the living room. She felt the heat of his hand on her waist and the pressure when he led her around. Luke was a great dancer. He pulled her closer and she could feel the warmth of his chest on her breasts.

Amber realized he was kidding, and she played along, but she was enjoying the dance and being in Luke's arms immensely.

Luke kept on humming and twirling her around. She finally realized that it was "Old MacDonald Had a Farm" and she burst out laughing.

"Why are you laughing while I'm trying to seduce you?"

"If you're trying to seduce me, why are you humming that song?"

"It just came to me."

"Okay. Sorry that I interrupted. Go ahead."

"Go ahead and do what?"

"Seduce me."

He shrugged. "I kind of lost the mood."

That was disappointing. She shouldn't have said anything. "You were on 'Old MacDonald had a cow.'"

He grinned slightly, but she knew she'd blown it. It was up to her to set things right. So she moved toward him, slipped her arms around his waist and gave him a kiss that would blast his boots off.

His lips were warm, his mouth open and inviting. She removed his cowboy hat and tossed it on the couch. Running her fingers through his hair, she drew him ever closer to her.

She just couldn't get enough of Luke.

When she broke the kiss, he said, "I promise I won't sing about Old MacDonald having a cow, if you kiss me like that again."

"Deal."

And she did.

Then Luke's cell phone rang and he looked at the Caller ID. "I'd better get this. It's Slim Gomez at the ranch."

"Go ahead." She needed to catch her breath anyway, but it was disappointing that the moment ended. But maybe it was for the best. He'd go back to the PBR, and she'd be working out of town.

Luke swore under his breath. "Are you kidding me? Dammit. No way. I'll be right over."

"Something wrong, Luke?"

"Let's just say that Old Luke Beaumont lost five more cows and two broncs, E-I-E-I-O."

Chapter Fifteen

"I'll go with you, Luke."

"We'll take my truck. It'll drive over anything."

Amber shook her head. "Aaron didn't have a chance to even plant his Sooner cap. He was going to do it tomorrow while he worked."

He opened the squeaky, rusted door to his truck and Amber got in. At least Luke had cleaned the inside and only a new battery was needed.

"It'll be interesting to see what Chapman artifact will be placed at the scene this time," Amber said. "Since Aaron didn't get a chance to 'lose' his cap."

He grunted.

"Luke, let me investigate, will you? And I'd like to speak with Slim once and for all. I haven't been able to touch base with him yet. I want his version of what happened each time, and I'll take a statement from him downtown."

"Fine with me, but you don't suspect Slim, do you?"

She shrugged. "No one is off my list."

"Not even me?" Luke asked.

She winked. "No way. You probably had your stock insured and are after the payout."

Luke slapped his forehead with a hand and his hat went flying.

"I knew I forgot something important—insurance!"

"Are you serious, Luke?"

"It's too expensive to insure all of the stock."

"You didn't even insure your fancy breeding stock and some horses?"

"Nope. We musketeers are a little cash poor right now."

"Musketeers?" she asked.

"One for all and all for one," Luke said. "My brothers."

Pulling up to the ranch, he said, "There's Slim now." Luke pointed. "Over there. You can see him by the light on the outside of the barn."

"I know Slim. We did a lot of talking back and forth when Big Dan was an absentee owner. Do you mind if I do the questioning?"

"Suit yourself, Sergeant."

"Thank you." She laughed. "I know how it'll pain you to keep quiet. And, Luke?"

"Yeah?"

"I'm really sorry. I promise that I'll get to the bottom of this."

They exited the truck and Amber felt an overwhelming sense of guilt. She should have done surveillance for the last couple of nights, but instead she'd been playing house with Luke.

She'd had to work until eleven, but after that she could have hidden out and watched the northeast pasture. But she was getting ahead of herself...

"Slim, what's the story? Did the rustlers use the northeast pasture again?" she asked.

"*Sí.*"

Slim looked like he'd rather be anywhere else than talking to her.

She leaned against Luke's truck and wrote in a small notebook. "They have a lot of guts using the same pasture and the same exit."

"Sí."

"Slim, who put livestock in the northeast pasture in light of the rustling going on?" she asked.

"Me. I never thought it would happen again. Never. Or I wouldn't have done it."

"You sure?" she asked. "Are you sure you're not helping the rustlers?"

"Amber! What are you saying?" Luke stepped in between the two. "Slim is a long-term employee of the Beaumont Ranch. He's my ramrod."

"Luke, you horse's butt, go away, and let me talk to Slim. Then the three of us are going to walk the route that the truck took. Find more flashlights, please."

"Yes, Sergeant," Luke said.

After Luke had left, she turned back to Slim. "I hope you understand that everyone's a suspect, Slim. That's how I work."

"Sí."

Amber got a couple more *"Sí'*s" out of Slim but, basically, he looked like a deer caught in the headlights.

Amber lowered her voice in an attempt to calm him. "Slim, you're acting like you're scared. Why?"

He shrugged. "I just have a lot on my mind and I should have moved the stock to a different pasture. It's my fault."

"What else is on your mind, partner?" Luke asked, returning from getting flashlights.

"My little girl, Luisa. She's been sick."

"Sick?" Amber asked. She hated to hear that. "She's about eight years old, isn't she?"

Slim looked on the brink of tears. "She is ten. Yes. Very sick."

"Don't beat yourself up, Slim, about turning out the stock into the same pasture. Let's find out who did this."

Luke handed out the flashlights. "Let's go."

It was quite a jarring ride to the northeast pasture, about a mile, over uneven terrain, but it was the perfect evening. They found the truck tracks and shone their flashlights.

"What's that?" she asked. "On the right. Over there."

They walked over to inspect the object.

"It's a jar," Amber said. "Like the type used for moonshine." She slipped into her gloves, put a pencil into the jar and lifted it. "Smells like someone just drank out of it. It's pretty fresh." She dropped it into a glassine evidence bag. "More Chapman litter. I really have to talk to my brothers about trashing the countryside. A person littering in Oklahoma can be fined between $200 and $5,000 and jailed for up to thirty days."

"Ouch," Luke said. "But how do we know it's a Chapman hooch jar?"

"It has a C on the bottom in red paint," Slim noted.

Amber laughed. "Of course! C was a good year."

Slim shook his head. "You aren't taking this very seriously, Sergeant Chapman."

"Oh, I am, Slim. I definitely am."

"Aren't you worried that your family did this...stealing, Sergeant?" Slim asked.

She shrugged. "To find three things on the scene that belong to my family seems awful coincidental. If they were the thieves, they wouldn't be that stupid."

Slim shook his head. "*Sí*, but it seems that they are guilty to me."

She had another idea. "If we find another thing that belongs to the Chapmans on the scene, I'd definitely be convinced of their guilt." She turned to Luke and gave him a clandestine wink.

"I'd be convinced, too, Amber. In fact, if one more thing is found that can be identified as belonging to a member of your family, I'd say that it would be time to make an arrest."

"Absolutely," she agreed. "And I can't wait to do it. We'll have a Chapman wing at the jail."

Luke chuckled. "I thought there was already a Chapman wing at the jail."

"You are so totally funny...*not*!" Amber said. She'd be more serious, but there were just too many Chapman items planted to make the scene believable. Her family wouldn't be that stupid.

"Slim, back to you. I know that the Beaumonts' staging and loading area is on the northeast pasture, and that the trucks have forever taken the same route on the side of the junkyard back to the highway—that's why the high grass is tamped down. And Ronnie's bandanna was found on those bushes. Kyle's pocketknife was found on the tracks down there. And the Chapman shine jar was found over there." She pointed to each area.

Slim shrugged his shoulders. "I do not know, Sergeant Chapman. I was not present when you found them."

"Yes. This is true," Amber said. "And, Slim, whenever you put stock out in the northeast pasture, the stock disappears."

"Yes, but I will stop."

"No. Don't do anything different. We don't want to spook the rustlers," Amber said.

"I HAVE AN IDEA," Amber said as they walked to Luke's truck to drive to her apartment.

"What is it?"

"First, I'm going to tell Aaron to lose his hat tomorrow after all. And tomorrow night, we are going to do a little surveillance."

"I take it that you suspect Slim?"

"Yes."

"Dammit, I hope not." Slim was a trusted member of the Beaumont family and was given everything he asked for. Slim wouldn't steal from them.

"You'd rather that I suspect my family?" she asked.

"Yes. I mean no. I mean yes."

Amber raised an eyebrow. "So which one is it?"

"Aw...hell. I don't know."

"I know that Slim has been a friend to your family forever, but sometimes good people do bad things for a reason. I'm going to find out that reason as soon as I can," Amber said.

Her phone rang. "Hello?"

"It's Fitz."

"Yes, Captain?"

"Big Dan Beaumont just walked out of the hospital. He's headed to his ranch."

"How? What?" Amber asked.

"He put on his street clothes and hitched a ride from a friend of his, Brian Redding. He convinced Brian that he was just at the hospital visiting when his car broke down."

"Obviously, Brian Redding didn't know Big Dan's recent history."

"Are you with Luke?"

"Yes, sir. I am. We're headed for my apartment."

"No. You're not."

"That's just what I said, Cap. I was absolutely *not* going to my apartment with Luke."

"You're going to find Big Dan, pick him up and bring him to jail. His probation officer Matty Matthews and his wife, Jill, happened to be out with Judge Bascom and Lena Bascom. Matty got a violation of probation typed up and signed in record time, along with a warrant. I have both in my hand."

"I'll let Luke know. He'll be totally disappointed. His father was doing fairly well."

"He shouldn't have walked out of the hospital without prior permission from his probation officer," Captain Fitzgerald said.

"Yeah."

"Okay, Amber. I'm gone," the captain said.

"Bye."

She hesitated before telling Luke of her phone conversation.

"That was Captain Fitz."

"Let me guess," he said. "My father walked out of the hospital. We have to pick him up. Where is he?"

"Not sure, but it seems that he's headed to his ranch. I mean your ranch. Judge Bascom ordered him picked up on a warrant. I drew the short straw."

"Let's go."

"No way. I'll drop you off at my apartment," she said.

"Are you forgetting that we are in my truck?"

Amber blinked. She had so much on her mind, she was losing it. "Oh! How did that happen?"

"I understand, Amber. With everything going on, I

feel like I'm being pulled into a million places. I have the ranch, my dad, the rustlers…what's next?" He rubbed his forehead, thinking how happy he felt with Amber by his side and how they were working together. "What were we talking about?"

Amber grinned. "I said that my truck can get over any terrain."

"That's right."

Amber thought for a while. "Why do you think Big Dan suddenly violated his probation?"

"My guess? He's sober enough to want to check out what I've been doing to his ranch. But I hate to see him arrested. He was doing okay, but I don't want him wandering around with a bum heart, although the doctor said that his stent operation was a success. Two stents in his chest and one in his leg."

Amber grinned. "He's better than new."

"He's probably feeling his oats, and now he wants to fight."

"You must have a lot on your mind, too, like your father and your missing stock," she said. "And winning the PBR Finals in November. And spending all your money to get the ranch in shape."

"And wondering if our long-term ramrod is guilty of stealing Beaumont stock."

"And wondering if the Chapmans are the good guys or the bad guys," Amber added.

They drove in silence for a while, each lost in their own thoughts.

Suddenly, Amber shouted, "Hey, look!" She pointed to a large stock truck. "Isn't that my father driving that thing?"

"Sure is!" Luke beeped his horn and Marv Chapman beeped back and waved.

"What on earth?" Amber couldn't make any sense out of why her father would be driving a stock truck. He didn't have any animals.

"What's he doing with that kind of truck?" Amber's throat was dry and she could barely breathe. "You don't think that…"

"Yes. I do."

"Motion for him to pull over, Luke."

"Okay."

Before Luke could stop his truck entirely, Amber was out and running.

"Dad? What's this?" she asked.

"A stock truck. What does it look like?"

"But why do you have a stock truck? You don't have any stock."

"I know. But I got a great deal on it."

Amber shone her flashlight on the truck. It needed a cleaning, due to manure and whatnot. There was fresh mud on the tires, which might be from the Beaumonts' northeast pasture.

"Who did you buy it from?" she asked.

"A couple of guys from Tennessee. They posted a notice at Porky's Feed and Grain. I pulled the little paper off with their phone number on it, and I gave them a call. We met at Tommy Lang's bar and did the exchange. Anything else, Sergeant?"

"Did you get a bill of sale?" she asked.

"Amber, this isn't my first rodeo. Of course I did."

"Can I see it?"

He pulled a piece of paper out of his pocket and handed it to her. She looked at it quickly. "When did you buy it?"

"Just last night."

"I'll study the bill of sale later."

"What's going on, Amber? Why are you so concerned about my truck?"

"More Beaumont stock has been rustled. This time they took a couple of Luke's prize bucking broncs, along with five more head."

"So you think that because I got this stock transport truck that I rustled Beaumont stock?"

"I don't, Dad, but you got to admit that suddenly driving around in one of these things is a little out of the ordinary."

"I drive around in a lot more unusual vehicles in my junk business, but this isn't for junk. I'm going to use it," he said. "With a couple of modifications."

"For what?"

"You'll see."

"I gotta go, Dad. I'll see you later."

"Where're you going at this late hour?"

"I can't say, Dad. It's business."

"Be careful, daughter."

She nodded and walked back to Luke's truck. Amber sank into the seat. "I feel like Alice who just fell through the rabbit hole. I suppose you'd like to know what my father is doing with a stock truck."

"It crossed my mind," he snapped.

"Now, don't go getting all suspicious. He said he bought it from some guys from Tennessee just today." She pulled out the bill of sale and smoothed it out.

"So if you believe your father that he just bought it, then the guys from Tennessee are the rustlers."

"Look, he has a bill of sale." She held the paper up to him.

"You know that doesn't mean much until you can verify it."

"I believe my father."

"Of course you would. But let's drop the subject of your father for now and pick on mine." He was quiet for a while then blurted, "What's with these fathers of ours?"

Amber shrugged. "Beats me, but I'm asking you to keep an open mind."

"Your father has a stock transport truck, there's Chapman stuff all over the scene, and I'm supposed to keep an open mind?"

"Luke, you are kidding, right? I thought we agreed that the evidence was being planted. Don't let me down, please. I've ruled them out."

"I thought so, too, until your father showed up with a stock truck."

"Let me handle this investigation! Don't jump to conclusions," she snapped.

He was quiet for a while, then said, "You're right, of course, and I don't want to fight with you." He held out his arms, and Amber leaned into them and laid her head on his shoulder."

"I don't want this investigation to come between us."

"Neither do I, but I have a feeling that before everything is over, we'll be fighting again," Luke said.

"I prefer to think of us as having an intellectual disagreement rather than a fight."

"Call it what you want. The results are the same."

Chapter Sixteen

They drove down the long, bumpy road that led to the Beaumont Ranch.

"I don't recognize that bright yellow truck," Luke said.

"If it has five different toucans on the back end and a big cheeseburger, it's Brian Redding's. He thinks he's the Jimmy Buffet of Beaumont," Amber said.

Luke chuckled. "Right now, he's the getaway driver for Big Dan, absconder."

"Do you see your father anywhere?"

Luke pointed. "He's walking to the barn. He's alone."

"And here comes Brian Redding," Amber said. "Which one do you want?"

"I'll take my father," Luke said, getting out of his truck.

"I'll get rid of Brian, and absolve him of all guilt. He'll like that. Then I'll send him on his way." Amber took a deep breath. "Luke, when you catch up with your father, don't mention the warrant, please."

"I won't. Musketeer promise."

"Gee, I would have just taken a little pinky swear, but you jumped right to the major musketeer promise," she joked. "When you find him, bring Big Dan to me."

"He's all yours," Luke said. "Oh, for how long?"

She shrugged. "I'm guessing that the judge will give him a slap on the wrist when Dan tells him that he just wanted to check on things at his ranch."

"Meet you back here." Luke exited the truck and the darkness swallowed him up.

Amber took the keys out of the ignition and slipped them into her pocket. It was an extra precaution, just in case Big Dan was tempted to add car theft to his repertoire. Or in case Luke was tempted to help his father escape to somewhere.

Luke wouldn't dare!

She had to get back to those two.

It was strange being back on a ranch that wasn't even hers but that she loved since she was a little girl. Could it be the very place her family might have stolen stock from?

Quickly, she knocked on the driver's-side window of the yellow truck. Brian Redding was watching a DVD.

"Hi, Brian."

He flashed a dazzling smile. "Sergeant Chapman! How nice to see you."

"You, too. But there's a little problem here. Big Dan should have never left the hospital. He's a patient there. I'll see to it that he gets back. You can feel free to leave."

"You sure?" Brian asked. "It's no trouble to take him back there."

"I'm sure. Go ahead. Have a nice evening."

"Thanks."

She hurried over to the Beaumonts. She trusted Luke to bring his father in. It was Big Dan whom she didn't trust.

Luke walked toward her...alone.

"Where did he go, Luke?"

"Dammit! I turned my head just once and he was gone."

"We'll go around the barn. You take the left and I'll take the right. Meet you out back," Amber said.

"Then we'll go inside and check in there. Maybe he'll head for my truck and make another getaway."

Amber chuckled. "He can try, but he won't go far. I took the keys."

"Brilliant."

They walked around the barn as planned, each one calling his name. But when they met, neither of them had found Big Dan Beaumont.

"Dammit, Dad!" Luke shouted. "I'm hot and tired and have to get up early to get back here. Now, show yourself and quit being such a chicken."

"Same goes for me, Mr. Beaumont. No more games. Okay?"

"What kind of games are *you* playing, Sergeant?" asked Big Dan.

Amber whirled around and pointed her flashlight toward the sound of his voice. Big Dan had gained some weight since the last time she'd seen him in court, but he was still just a shadow of what he'd looked like when Valerie Lynn was alive.

"You didn't answer my question. What kind of games are you playing?"

"No games, Mr. Beaumont. I'll tell you straight. You've violated your probation by leaving the hospital. Your probation officer, Matty Matthews, is quite upset. So is Judge Bascom. There is a warrant out for your arrest. I have to take you to jail."

"I ain't going."

Amber took a deep breath. "Um, yes. Yes, you are."

It had been difficult arresting Big Dan. She knew how much he and Valerie Lynn did for the whole town, and it was hard to watch an icon fall, but it was her job, and she was going to arrest him.

"Not until the work is stopped here," he said, arms crossed.

"Are you still singing that same tune, Dad?" Luke stepped into the circle of light. "There're a lot of people who are helping us fix up the place. They all care, and you don't."

"That's their problem. No one told them to care," Big Dan shouted.

Amber pulled out her handcuffs. "You sound like a broken record, Mr. Beaumont. Now, put your hands behind your back."

"No."

"Dad, do what Amber tells you to do," Luke said.

"No."

"Dad, quit feeling sorry for yourself. A lot of people have lost a loved one. Jesse, Reed and I lost our mother. What gives you the monopoly on grieving? We want to save the place. If you're not with us, you're against us."

"Luke, Luke…this ranch killed your mother."

"An accident killed my mother. It wasn't the ranch's fault. It wasn't the horse's fault. It just happened. It was her time to go, and God called her home. That's what happened, Dad, and she'd never want to see you like this."

"God called her home," Big Dan whispered.

Luke nodded. "Yes."

That little sentence seemed to light a spark inside Big Dan's heart.

"I'll go peaceably, Sergeant."

Thank goodness, he'd been able to say the right words

to reach Big Dan or else his father was finally ready to hear them.

"I'd appreciate that, Mr. Beaumont. Please turn around and put your hands behind your back."

"Amber, is that really necessary?" Luke asked hating to see his father handcuffed. He remembered the old days when his parents were so happy together. He'd always wanted a love like they had.

He looked at Amber. She was someone special. She was independent like his mother, yet had a soft heart like she had.

"I'm so sorry, Luke, I have to. It's department policy."

Big Dan turned around, hands together behind his back. "Let Sergeant Chapman do her job, Luke. It's okay. I'm used to it."

"I don't want you to be used to it, Dad. I want this to be the last time. The town used to look up to you, and now you're a laughingstock. This isn't you, Dad."

Amber nodded. "I agree, but I'd like to add that everyone remembers how things used to be when the Beaumont Ranch was in its glory. They are proud of it, but more than that, everyone wants you to get help."

Amber put the cuffs on Big Dan Beaumont and led him to Luke's truck. She gently helped him into the back seat. Luke got into the driver's seat and held his hand out for the keys. Amber dropped them into his palm.

In the back, Big Dan Beaumont kept mumbling, "God called Valerie Lynn home. She wouldn't like to see me like this."

Luke started his truck. "Well, Amber, we just arrested my father—isn't it about time we arrest yours?"

"I HAVEN'T FINISHED my investigation, Luke, and you know it."

Amber slammed the door that led to the cells at the back of the sheriff's department. Big Dan Beaumont had been arrested, printed and given his one phone call. He'd passed on the call, but gotten a cell to himself since he was pending court transport, but primarily because no one else was in the Beaumont County lockup.

Luke shrugged. "Yeah, well, let's finish the damn thing. You wanted to talk to Slim again. We'll let's do it."

"No. I'd like to do some surveillance as soon as possible. I think that the rustlers know that we're wise to them, and they might make one last attempt. We told Slim to continue to load the northeast pasture, so I'm going to see what might happen. And, Luke, I'm going to draw the line. I don't want you with me for this."

"What if there's trouble?"

"I can handle trouble," she said.

Just then, the door burst open and a wide-eyed, disheveled kid of about sixteen wearing a uniform stood with his arms outstretched.

"Help. A lady is having a baby. Now. At Beaumont Breakfast and Burgers across the street. Help."

"Did you call 9-1-1?" Amber asked.

"They can't get the ambulance started."

"Dammit!" Luke exclaimed.

"Let's go," Amber said. "Luke, you can help me."

They both ran across the street. The door was held open by the same overwhelmed teen.

Amber spotted the mother-to-be in a booth at the back of the restaurant. She was a young, tiny woman of no more than seventeen. She was crying. A young man, about the same age, was patting her hand. He looked on the verge of tears, too.

"Luke, call Donny. Donny Cushman. Tell him to bring his hearse over here. Pronto!"

"Where's the manager of this place?" Amber asked. "Ask him or her to come over and see me."

Amber knelt down. "What's your name, honey?"

"Tiffany McCall."

"Well, Tiffany. I'm hoping to get you to the hospital. Think you can hold on?"

She shrugged, then cried out.

A nervous kid with tattoos on his neck and smelling of onions, bent and whispered, "I'm Johnny, one of the managers. Johnny…uh…Vanderhaven."

Amber looked up. Was everyone at Beaumont Breakfast and Burgers under seventeen?

"Johnny, clear your customers out of here, please."

Luke slid his cell phone into a case on his belt. "I'll herd them out, Amber. Johnny looks a little…paralyzed. And Donny Cushman is on his way. So are the EMTs. They're driving here in their own cars."

"Thanks, Luke. Think you can find something more to cushion Tiffany's head and back?"

"I saw a pile of new aprons," Luke said and took off running. She could hear the *thunk* of his boots on the marble floor. For some reason, it was comforting.

It wasn't as if she delivered a baby at Beaumont Breakfast and Burgers every day. She'd had training on delivering babies, but it was still scary.

Amber took a peek at Tiffany's status. Poor little thing. She was so tiny. She wished Donny would get here in his hearse.

"Where is everyone?" she asked Luke. "I think Tiffany is ready to pop."

"Lots of traffic, due to homecoming and freshman orientation events at the university. Something must be just beginning or maybe it's just letting out."

"It figures."

"Luke, call the office. Emily, the dispatcher, will answer. Tell her to get the fire department to help Donny Cushman's hearse get here."

Amber went back to dabbing the sweat off of Tiffany's face, letting the young woman squeeze her hand, and telling the man with her not to worry.

Amber was worrying enough for both of them.

Luke shook his head. "Amber, according to the dispatcher, there are two deputies who are on duty, and one by the name of Ron Rexall is on his way."

She sighed. "Good." She didn't take her eyes off of Tiffany.

Amber knew that Ron Rexall would help her if the EMTs didn't arrive in time and if she couldn't get ahold of a doctor. While she was waiting, she might as well try the doctor.

She blotted the girl's upper lip. "Luke, call the hospital. I want to talk to the ob-gyn on duty. Wait a minute."

"Tiffany, do you go to a doctor at the hospital?"

"I go to the free clinic there. Dr. Hill."

"Good. Luke?"

"I'm calling the hospital now, Amber. Dr. Hill. I take it that you want the doctor to help you deliver the baby if necessary?"

"You got it. And thanks, Luke."

Tiffany screamed and squeezed Amber's hand so hard Amber was surprised at the girl's strength. She looked over at Tiffany's boyfriend. He was enjoying a burger. She'd told him not to worry, but eating was just too much.

"Hey, put that down and hold her hand," Amber ordered.

Luke tapped a button on his cell and put it on speaker. "Amber, here's Dr. Hill."

"Dr. Hill, this is Amber Chapman of the Beaumont County Sheriff's Department. I am with Tiffany McCall, and we're sending her to you if the hearse arrives in time to transport her because the ambulance is down again. Tiffany seems ready to deliver."

Amber sighed in relief. Donny was here with his hearse and the EMTs arrived with some volunteer firefighters. Soon Tiffany and her boyfriend were on their way to the hospital. Amber updated Dr. Hill, who stated that he would be ready and waiting for her.

Crisis averted. The diner was blissfully silent.

Amber plopped into a booth, and Luke sat down opposite her and held her hands in his.

"You did a great job," he said.

Amber shook her head. "I couldn't have done it without you, you know. We make a good team."

His hands were strong and calloused. They were the hands of a working cowboy.

"We sure do. I've thought exactly that for a long time now," he said.

"You have?"

In answer, he kissed her hand.

Amber thought about the baby that young Tiffany was going deliver, and a wave of sadness washed over her. She looked at their joined hands. She just knew in her heart of hearts that Luke would make a great father and a thoughtful and caring husband.

She squeezed his hand. "You're the best, Luke. You really are."

"I like you a lot, Amber. Do you know that?"

"I think I do. And the feeling's mutual."

"How many?" Luke asked.

Was he asking what she thought he was asking?

"How many what?" She held her breath.

He smiled. "How many children would you like?"

"As many as I'm blessed with, but under six." She laughed.

"Just what I was thinking!"

THE NEXT EVENING, Amber looked at the quiet scene in front of her with her night-vision goggles. Luke's cattle stood peacefully in the northeast pasture. From her vantage point, she could see her father's house in the distance. All looked calm there. Lights were dim and someone had probably fallen asleep watching the TV.

"You are amazing, Amber."

"You have to be more specific." She laughed.

"You know what I'm talking about. You were cool and collected when it looked like Tiffany was going to deliver in the diner. You didn't blink an eye, and now you're here watching for rustlers. You're like a diamond, Amber. You have a lot of facets."

She shrugged. "Thank goodness I had a lot of help. And who knew that Donny Cushman was a maternity nurse in a past life? And Dr. Hill was at the clinic. Luckily, everything fell into place."

"But it could've gone bad for Tiffany." Luke shook his head. "We need that ambulance working. Hell, we need two new ambulances and the proper equipment."

"*We*? Sounds as if you're getting to be part of the town again, Luke."

"You know, it's not a bad town. Everyone comes together when needed, and you made me feel like I was needed back here, and I was."

"It didn't take me long to convince you to come back. Actually, you didn't have a choice. I bossed you around like a new recruit." She chuckled. "But, seriously, Luke, I don't know what I would have done if you weren't there to help me with Tiffany. I mean it."

"You would have done just fine." He was quiet for a while. "You know, Beaumont won't be the same without you when you leave."

"Beaumont will be fine without me. Captain Fitz will hire a new person off the list, and he or she will do a great job."

He shrugged. "Not like you. You can make an arrest, deliver a baby and then be here in the dirt working an investigation. In between, you're planning the rodeo and who knows what else."

"I'm planning breakfast right now. I'm in the mood for French toast and bacon. What about you?"

Luke smiled. "You're changing the subject, but I'll make breakfast. You've had a big day."

"So have you. It's not every day you help arrest your own father. I'm used to it, but it must have been a bit of a shock to you."

Luke grunted. "Big Dan just has to learn the hard way, I guess."

"Just talking to him the little time I had, I think that your dad is lonely. Just plain lonely. With your mother gone and you three riding with the PBR, he's just rattling around in that big house full of memories, it's not comforting him. I think that he equates the house with his happiness. Maybe he thinks that if the house is gone, he can be happy again."

"I think you're right," Luke said. "I've been thinking along the same lines. I think that the upcoming rodeo will do Dad a world of good. All three of us will be home, and it'll be like the old days when the Beaumont Ranch used to have annual rodeos and a barbecue. Dad can form new memories."

"But speaking of family, what's going on at the junk-yard?"

She looked down from her perch on the hill. "What the hell?"

The big overhead doors were all up now and it seemed that her brothers were pressure washing something inside. What puzzled her was that the garage bays were empty when they were usually packed to overflowing with parts and whatnot. There was no sign of her father's stock truck.

"Where is he with that truck?" she asked, her pulse pounding in her ears.

Luke looked through binoculars. "There he is over there. Driving on the side road of my northeast pasture."

"My father is not a rustler. My father makes illegal booze. Let's get it straight, please." She laughed nervously.

"Afraid not. He's branching out. He's going to load my stock into that trailer of his. Dammit, Amber. Why did it have to be your father?"

"Oh, no, Luke. It can't be. It just can't be!" Amber looked through her goggles. "Don't jump to conclusions, Luke. Although I should take my own advice."

They waited until the driver finally got out of the truck.

"No. It's Slim!" Luke said. "Let's go. I want to ask Slim what I ever did to him that caused him to steal from me, from my family."

"I know it's a shock to you, Luke." Amber put a hand on his arm. "But wait. Let's see if he has an accomplice."

No one else showed to help him, and Slim began herding cattle from the pasture into the transport truck.

"C'mon, Amber! I just can't stand here any longer. Let's rock."

"I have to ask you to let me go first, and you need to let me do the talking. Or how about if you just stay here and wait for me?"

"That's not going to happen."

"Just stay behind me, then."

"That isn't going to happen, either," he mumbled, but Amber could hear him clearly.

They walked toward the truck and when she got closer, she called his name. "Slim. Slim Gomez. It's Sergeant Amber Chapman. I'd like to talk to you."

Slim raised his hands in the air.

Amber made a motion with her hand. "You can put your hands down. You're not under arrest—yet."

"Dammit, Slim! Why?" Luke shouted. "If you needed money, why the hell didn't you ask for it? Why? Answer me!"

Slim kept his hands up. "Because, Luke, you weren't around, and I wasn't getting a salary for all the work I was doing. Your father wasn't paying me, and because my little Luisa is sick!"

It killed him to hear that. Luke stood as still as a statue. "What's wrong with Luisa?"

He adored that little girl. Ever since she had been old enough to stand, she'd follow him around, hoping that he'd put her on a horse and lead her around the paddock. She had to be ten years old by now.

"Leukemia. My little girl is sick, Luke. Seriously sick. Everything costs money, and the Beaumonts weren't paying me. I couldn't get a loan because I wasn't working. I didn't know what to do." Slim began to sob. "I only took what you owed me. I sold them at a good price and only take my regular pay for Luisa. The rest of the money, I set aside for Big Dan, but I can give it to you."

"Dammit, Slim, I don't care about that, but why the hell didn't you call me or Reed or Jesse and tell us what was goin' on?"

"I guess I got mad at you Beaumonts for ignoring us. I will not sell any more. I am sorry, Luke. I know I'm fired. I will pack up my family and will leave our house, er…your ramrod house. Please, can I have two weeks?"

"Aw…dammit, Slim. I feel like I've been sucker punched. You've worked for my family for over twenty years."

Slim finally lowered his hands. "That is the same question that I wanted to ask you or your papa. After working for Beaumonts for twenty-three years, why did he forget Slim and his family? Why?"

"Because Big Dan can't even take care of himself. He hasn't wanted the ranch since my mother died."

"I know that. But he didn't tell me to get another job. He just forgot my family and me."

"Slim, it seems like mistakes were made on both sides but, no, I don't want you to move. I don't want you to give up the ramrod house, and I am not going to fire you. I should, I really should, but I see your situation as our fault, too, so I'm going to give you another chance. We both have trust to regain."

"Gracias."

"There's more. I don't like the way you framed the Chapmans. You put their things around the area—was that to mislead Sergeant Chapman?"

"Yes. I am ashamed, and I apologize to Sergeant Chapman."

"If Luke can forgive you, I guess I can," she said,

"But I don't think you realize how much anguish you caused."

"I do. I am so very sorry." Slim wiped his eyes with the back of his sleeve.

Luke shook his head. "Slim, I want you to take care of your family and help us work on restoring the ranch and property. We are going to throw one of the biggest rodeos this county has seen in a long time, and I'm going to need you to make sure that the arena and grounds are in good shape for contestants and spectators. The position comes with an advance and a raise."

Slim pumped Luke's arm so fast, Amber thought that it was going to come out of its socket. *"Gracias. Muchas gracias.* Thank you, Luke." Fresh tears were starting. "I will unload the cattle."

"Whose cattle truck is that?" Amber asked.

"It belongs to the person that I've been selling cattle to."

"Who's that, Slim?" Amber asked.

"Please. They know nothing. I don't want to give their name. They think that they are helping you by buying your stock."

"I'll find out eventually, Slim. You can count on it, but for now, give the truck back, and tell whomever you've been selling the cattle to that there aren't any more available."

"*Sí*, Luke. I will do that immediately."

"And I'd like to visit Luisa. Is that okay with you?" Luke asked.

"*Sí*. She would like that." He pulled a bandanna from his jeans' pocket, wiped his eyes and blew his nose. "I am so sorry."

Amber waited until Slim was out of earshot before she chuckled. "Luke, I guess you won't be pressing charges."

"No. No way."

Amber was touched by Luke's kind, generous gesture. She probably wouldn't have been so forgiving, especially if the perpetrator happened to be her family, but she admired Luke. In fact, she wanted to kiss him right here, right now. What he did was like an aphrodisiac to all of her senses.

"I robbed you of your big case before you leave for the state police, didn't I?" Luke asked, opening the truck door for her.

"I solved it, so that's okay. But, better yet, I saw another side of you that I really admire. You're a good man, Luke Beaumont. Now, let's go to my apartment, and I'll cook us something."

"I'm not hungry for food, Amber. I'm hungry for you."

Chapter Seventeen

Amber chuckled. "What a line! Does that usually work for you?"

Luke's eyes twinkled. "It has worked like fine wine, but I only use it on very special occasions."

"You mean on very special buckle bunnies, don't you?"

"The buckle bunnies are usually too young for me. Besides, they go for Jesse or Reed."

"That's not what I observed, you stud you."

Luke turned left onto the highway and headed for her apartment.

"What about you, Amber? I haven't heard you speak of any special men in your life."

"That's because there hasn't been anyone special in a long time. There's been a couple of guys, but they take off sooner or later. I've just been waiting for that special one, I guess."

"And I've been waiting for that special woman, and I think I've found her. She's a cop, and she's very bossy, but she's incredible. I remember walking her home from the senior prom, and I've never really forgotten her."

"And my special guy is a bull rider. He cares about Beaumont, although he's never here. He's making a name for himself on the circuit. Then maybe he'll settle down in Beaumont."

"But I'd be settling down by myself. My prom queen will be leaving to spread her wings in a bigger piece of Oklahoma."

"But, Luke, we have another month together. We have until Labor Day."

"One month? Well, then, I'd better use my charm on you."

"It won't take much. You had me at 'I'm hungry for you.'"

Luke pulled into a parking space at the back of the Happy Tea Pot and they ran up the stairs. Amber had the key in her hand and she opened the door quickly.

Shoes were kicked off, clothes were scattered and two half-naked bodies hit the couch.

She was so excited that she wanted to scream to the world, "This is the guy I've waited for!"

Luke's lips teased Amber's. "Mmm, Luke. Kiss me."

Their tongues danced and their hands couldn't keep still.

"Mmm...Amber...finally."

"Kiss me, Luke. Hard." Amber was breathless, hot.

He kissed the mounds of her breasts. Amber slipped off the straps of her bra, and Luke undid the hooks in record time.

"You're beautiful, Amber."

"Thanks, Luke. So are you." She grinned. "Now let me see you get out of those jeans."

He did a little striptease that had her laughing and lusting for him.

When he got rid of his underwear, his length stood at attention.

"Got condoms, Luke?"

"Yeah, I'm packing."

"Come here," she whispered.

"I thought you'd never ask. But would you rather move to your bedroom?"

"No. This couch hasn't seen any action. When you go, I'd like to remember us making love whenever I see it."

"Then let's give you something to remember."

And he did.

IN THE MORNING, Luke turned to Amber. "Do you want to take a ride with me to see Luisa Gomez, Slim's daughter? I planned on visiting her."

Amber had to do something to stop from thinking. In the light of day, she remembered that she planned on moving. After what might be their last night together, she'd keep the memory of it forever.

"Sure. I remember Luisa somewhat. I go to the schools to teach Stranger Danger and safety and a couple of other things, and Luisa is such a bright girl, both in knowledge and demeanor. She told me that she wants to be a cop. But I have a feeling that if you came to school to speak, she'd want to be a bull rider."

"Bless her little heart," Luke said with such sincerity and caring that Amber felt her knees getting weak. "I'd like to stop at a store somewhere and get her some balloons, and maybe a toy. Maybe you could tell me what kind a girl would like."

"I'd love to. It's been a while since I've been a ten-year-old girl, but I think I can pick out something she'd like."

"Shall we go shopping?" Luke asked.

"Absolutely. Now, there's a man after my heart!"

"If you only knew."

She smiled. "I'll drive us."

"First one down wins." She took the stairs two at a time, but Luke sat on the metal railing and slid down. He hit the ground way before she did.

They drove to the Beaumont Emporium, which sold everything from buttons to milking machines.

"Luke! I have the perfect gift for Luisa. A tiny oven. She can bake little things like cakes and cupcakes. I wanted one when I was her age, but it never happened."

"You think she'd like an *oven*?"

"Believe me, she'll go crazy. Just call Slim and make sure she doesn't have one already."

He punched in numbers on his cell phone. "Hi, Slim, it's Luke. Yes, everything's okay. Just a quick question— does Luisa have one of those little ovens that she can bake with? Great. Okay. Yeah. Amber and I...we are going to visit her, and we thought we'd bring her a gift. Yes, we'll tell her that you and Juanita will be up to visit later. Sure."

Luke turned to Amber and gave her a thumbs-up. "It's a go on the oven."

"She'll love it, Luke. Believe me."

When they arrived at the hospital, they were asked to cover up with a gown and pants, a hairnet, gloves and a facemask, and nets to cover their shoes.

Amber's heart broke when she saw little Luisa and the other children gathered in the playroom. Most were attached to IV poles and several wires going from their little bodies to machines that beeped. Many of them had lost their hair. Luisa was one of them.

"Luisa!" yelled Luke, gently giving the girl a hug.

"And you're with Officer Amber!" She giggled. "Uncle Luke, is Officer Amber your bestest girlfriend?"

Amber bit her bottom lip so she wouldn't laugh. It seemed to her that all of Beaumont wanted to know the answer to that question.

"Uh…sure. Amber is my bestest girlfriend, just like you are, Luisa."

"Nice save," Amber mumbled then turned to Luisa. "Sweetie, would you like to help us pass out even more gifts? We'll be just like Santa Claus."

Luisa whispered, "Sure. Just like Santa, but I'm ten. Santa's for kids."

"I believe." Luke raised his hand as if taking an oath.

Amber did the same. "I believe."

Luisa giggled and raised her hand. Wires hung down and Amber's heart was breaking for what these little kids had to go through. "Okay. I believe, too."

They passed out balloons, and passed out dozens of books and toys for the other kids in the children's wing.

Luisa grinned. "You know, Uncle Luke, I watch you on TV. Well, when the TV wasn't broken, I did."

"It hasn't worked?" Luke asked. "For how long?"

"A long time," she replied. "We can't even play movies."

"Sweetie, expect a television by tomorrow. And one that plays movies."

Amber was falling even more for Luke. The man was a pushover for the kids. If one asked for a real car, he'd get it for them. "Expect a car by tomorrow," he'd say.

Little Luisa loved the stove, or at least the picture of it on the box. The head nurse said that the oven would have to go home due to a hospital safety hazard.

"I'm sorry, Uncle Luke and Officer Amber. I can't have my oven here."

Luke hugged Luisa. Amber could tell that he was afraid to hold her very tight, she was so fragile. "Don't worry about a thing, Luisa. We'll drop it off at your house, and you can use it when you get home. It'll be something that you can look forward to."

Amber's heart melted. Luke would be wonderful with children.

"Awesome," Luisa said. "I can't wait to get home and bake with my oven."

Luke let her go and smiled widely. "Your mom and dad send their love, and they'll be up later."

"Awesome," she repeated.

"You just get better, sweetie," Amber said. "And then we'll be over to your house to have a piece of cake that you baked in your little oven."

"Promise?"

"We promise." Luke crossed his heart.

Luisa looked from Luke to Amber, then back to Luke. "Will you visit me here again?"

"You know it!" Luke punched the air with a fist.

"Will you talk to the kids about how you ride bulls?" she asked.

"If you want me to, I will."

"And, Officer Amber, will you talk about how you arrest criminals?"

The fact that she'd almost arrested Luisa's father made Amber shudder. If it wasn't for Luke, Slim would be in jail at this moment.

If her little girl was in need of money to pay for her leukemia treatments, and if she were as desperate as Slim, she'd probably have done the same thing.

Luke made the right call not to prosecute.

Luke and Amber promised that they'd be back as soon as possible.

"And I never break a promise," added Luke.

"Amber, let's go to R.J.'s Major Appliances. I'm going to get those kids a TV or two."

"You got it!"

They got back in the truck and drove to R.J.'s about ten miles away. The ride gave them both time to reflect.

"Those kids break my heart," Amber said, tears brimming in her eyes. "But they're the strongest people I know."

"It'll be fun telling them about bull riding," Luke said.

"And law enforcement."

"You know, Amber, my bull riding pals would love to visit the kids. They're very generous with their time."

At R.J.'s, Luke didn't buy just one TV, he bought four of the biggest that R.J.'s had, along with a collection of cartoons and children's movies.

On the way to her apartment, Amber offered to buy the TVs. "Let me buy it all, Luke. You've been sinking all your money into the ranch. It'd be my pleasure. I want to do it for the children."

"No way. I have plastic. I can charge it."

"Luke, please, I insist. Let's not get all crazy over this. If you hadn't thought of it, I would have. The kids are in my heart, too. I'm only sorry that I haven't visited them before this. I'm feeling really guilty."

"Okay, Amber. I understand how you feel. I'm feeling a little guilty, too. Slim was right. The Beaumonts ignored their help—loyal people who have families and bills and…"

They pulled over to the side of the road and Amber took Luke's hand. Looking into his sky blue eyes, she said, "It's not your fault. Big Dan had his own problems and things to deal with. Slim knew that. He should have contacted you and told you the situation."

Luke ran a finger down her cheek. "He definitely should have. He could have left me a message through the PBR."

Amber rubbed the nape of his neck. "Or I could have gotten to you sooner. I meant to, but life got in the way. I meant to."

Kissing the back of her hand, Luke said. "When God passed out guilt, we got in line twice. Let's just say we're fixing things now, in more ways than one."

They pointed the truck toward her apartment over the Happy Tea Pot, and fifteen minutes later they were in Amber's bed.

"You have the strongest arms," she said, running her hands over his muscled biceps as he was poised over her.

"I love your blue eyes," she said. They were now deep with passion.

Luke kissed her nipples. "And I love looking at you— the way your hair fans out on the pillow, the way you look at me like I'm the greatest person on earth, the way you understand me…" He entered her and whispered, "And I love making love with you."

They made love so gently, so lovingly, and when it was all over, the beauty of it had tears pooling in Amber's eyes.

"Did I hurt you?" Luke said. "Tell me."

"No. Of course not. It's a happy cry," she said.

"That again?" He held her to him until they fell asleep.

THEY WOKE TO the sound of Luke's cell phone ringing.

"Is this important, Reed? I have something I'd like to do, then I'll call you back."

Disconnecting, he turned to Amber. "I don't think we're done yet, do you?"

"You read my mind," Amber said. She kissed his chest, his neck, and he groaned. She knew just the right spots that he liked, and he reciprocated.

"Amber," he whispered. "You're quite a woman. I liked how you handled the investigation, and loved how you interacted with the kids in the hospital. You're great with a hammer, and I love being with you."

He kissed her with all the love he felt in his heart, in his soul, and then with his body, he showed her.

LATER, HE SAT up and called Reed back as he chugged coffee in Amber's kitchen.

"Hey, Reed! How's it going?" Luke asked. "Where are you two musketeers?"

"Albany, New York. At the arena here. I won the go-round last night. Jesse won tonight. But this is the last event, Luke. We have money, and we're both coming home. We'll help you get ready for the Beaumont Ranch Rodeo."

"We're going to have a charity dance and barbecue the day before the rodeo and during it. All proceeds go to buying an ambulance or two."

"Terrific. Should be a blast. How's Dad?"

"Dad is sober, staying at the rehab facility without too much lip, and is opening up during group. I sign him out when he has furlough, and we go to the ranch. He looks over everything and picks up a hammer and does some work. He's opening up about Mom and is talking about being the guide for tours through the ranch."

"Good. Really good," Reed said.

"He's looking forward to seeing you both," Luke said. "He genuinely is. And your bedrooms will be ready. In fact, everything is going to be ready soon."

"Great, Luke. Great job."

"I couldn't have done it without my musketeers and without Amber Chapman. She's a special woman, a very special woman. See you soon, bro."

Amber came into the kitchen wrapped in a terry robe, but Luke knew that under that, she was wearing nothing. It wouldn't take much to loosen her belt and—

She looked on the verge of tears. "What's wrong, Amber?"

"I heard from the state police. I have to start there in five days."

"What about the Beaumont Ranch Rodeo? What about the barbecue? What about us?"

Tears pooled in Amber's eyes. "We knew that there was no us. We knew it right from the beginning. You're going on the PBR circuit. I'm going to work for the state police. Even if you win the Finals, that won't be enough for you. You'll want to win it again and you'll go back. You love riding with your brothers and all the other cowboys."

"Yeah, but I love *you* more. I'd give up riding for you."

She shook her head. "I'd never ask you to give up riding."

She blinked and tears ran in small rivulets down her cheeks. "Oh, Luke, I love you, too, but I don't see how a long-distance relationship would work. We are both going to throw ourselves into our careers, and that'll be it. It was good while it lasted, but we both knew that it would end. Maybe not so soon, but we both knew there was a deadline. We'll both do fine. You'll see."

"So, that's it, huh? That's how you feel? You love me but goodbye?" Luke asked, feeling empty inside. He didn't understand why she didn't want to work at their relationship. "Does this have anything to do with the other guys leaving you? So this way, you'll leave me first?"

"Don't be ridiculous."

Luke thought he might have struck a nerve. "So I'm being ridiculous, huh?"

"Yes."

"Maybe you're right, Amber. Who are we kidding? No sense even trying to see each other. No sense keeping our relationship going."

"We had a good time, Luke."

"Are you saying we just had a fling, nothing more? Just a good time? Just good sex?"

She bit her lip. He knew that was not what she really thought—she said that she loved him—but she just wanted a clean break. Okay. If that's what she wants—

He drained his cup of coffee. "So I'm being ridiculous, and I was just a fling?" She couldn't mean that; she was just running away for some reason.

"It wasn't like that, Luke. It's just that we are going separate ways. We have our dreams to fulfill."

"I'll be out of your apartment tomorrow," Luke said, feeling numb. "The ranch house is livable and mold-free."

"Livable? For how long?"

"About a week."

"And you didn't move?"

"I didn't want to, Amber. I've been really happy here with you."

"Now we have no choice. We are both packing up to move."

"Dammit, Amber, you sure move fast."

"I have to move fast."

"Where are you going to live?"

"At an extended stay hotel for now. They sent me a

list of places." She looked around. "I'm going to hate to leave this apartment when I get hired permanently. I really love it. I wonder if there's a way I can keep it. Maybe my mother would like to move in here. Or maybe—"

"You've spent more time planning what to do with your apartment than you've spent planning anything about us, but I can take a hint."

Amber had already decided that their relationship wasn't worth working at, so then why was he acting like a lovesick bull?

"Luke, I'll continue to work on your rodeo up until the point when I step into my car. And you can always call me on my cell phone if you need help."

"Don't worry. My brothers will pick up the slack."

"They'll have to because I have to work all weekends until further notice. I'll be shadowing another officer. That means that I won't even be able to attend the barbecue or the rodeo."

Luke was speechless. Finally he said, "Gee, that's too bad because I was hoping you'd be the announcer. From what I understand those attending want to see me ride, so I was going to ride."

"That's too bad, Luke. I would have announced."

"Not necessary now. You take care of packing up and getting ready to leave. I'll take care of the rodeo plans," he said. "Oh, and, Amber, when you pack, don't forget the couch. And when you look at it, think of us and how we made love on that couch!"

AMBER DROVE UP Interstate 87 north toward Spirit Springs to start her job with the Oklahoma State Police. She tried listening to talk radio, but it made her want to scream. She trolled the dial until she found a country station.

Turning up the music, she sang at the top of her lungs just so she wouldn't have to think.

Her thoughts intruded anyway.

She didn't want to think about how her life was changing, how she was going to miss her crazy family and friends, how she would miss the rodeo, and there were many, many more things she'd miss.

Above all, she was going to miss Luke. Maybe she had left him before he could leave her. She'd cared for him since as far back as she could remember, and she'd always look for him to visit Beaumont. Much to her dismay, his visits had been few and far between, and he always left for the PBR.

She would follow him on TV. And listen to any gossip or bits of information about him. How strange was that?

She'd wanted Luke and she'd had him. They'd lived together for several glorious weeks. They'd worked together; they'd solved the rustling problem together.

They'd made love.

When she'd told him about leaving early for her new job, she hadn't felt happy, and this was a job she'd been wanting for six years or more.

She was going to miss the Beaumont Ranch Rodeo. There hadn't been a rodeo for at least three years.

It had always been the hit of the town, a fund-raiser for things like ambulances and fire trucks, and it was during the rodeo that the Beaumont brothers came home. She'd even worked on this rodeo and loved being a part of it, but now she couldn't even attend.

She'd blown it. She'd blown it big time with Luke.

But she was going to give this job a chance. She owed that to herself.

LUKE HAD HELPED Amber put some things into her car. Since she'd let him stay in her apartment, it was the least he could do for her.

Then he watched her drive away out of his life.

He liked how she always rolled up her sleeves and pitched right in, helping with the ranch, helping with the rodeo, working hard to catch who was rustling his cattle. She helped his father; she wasn't scared to deliver a baby; she could cook and bake like a pro.

He missed making love with her. Hell, he missed just being with her, and she'd only been gone two days.

Amber had continued to surprise him on a daily basis, but her biggest surprise was how she'd cut him loose. She'd hurt him badly and he couldn't even talk to her and reason with her. She'd closed herself off.

He still believed that she was afraid he'd leave her first, but he'd had no intention of doing that. He'd thought they could work out something with their schedules, once she knew hers, but she hadn't even been willing to do that.

But he wasn't going to give up on Amber. No way.

He was just going to give her some space to figure out what she really wanted.

LUKE WAS BUSY with the Friday night barbecue. Smokin' Sammy's House of Hickory was setting up, so that should have been it, but Luke had scrambled to rent picnic tables from Oklahoma City, so he hoped that they'd get there in time.

He'd also ordered a bunch of tables and chairs along with a bunch of umbrellas.

The bounce house was up and ready. A lime green

castle loaded with colorful balls was ready, too. The kids would have a great time.

Slim Gomez had groomed the shrubs and the lawn to show off the native flowers he'd planted.

The ranch house was done. The barns were done. Slim's house was done. Some of the outbuildings needed help yet, like the bunkhouse, but his brothers were available to help with the construction now, if they ever stopped sleeping and became vertical. Those musketeers were pooped.

However, his brothers had come through with a lot of money. They rode hot on the summer circuit.

And it was cool to watch his father coming alive again. Big Dan truly enjoyed helping the historical association that gave tours of the ranch and grounds and lectured about the history of the Beaumont Ranch. His father added to the lectures by telling colorful stories about the prior ranch residents.

Smokin' Sammy had his smokers going and the smell wafted through the air. It'd bring buyers to the barbecue as if they were in a trance.

Everything should be ready just as soon as the rental truck came with the picnic tables and extra tables and chairs.

When the truck just arrived, Luke sprang into action. He helped the guys to position the picnic tables and set up the other tables, chairs and umbrellas.

Everything was in place except for one person: Amber. Luke wanted Amber at his side. After all, he couldn't have done half of this without her taking care of publicity and photos and lots of little details.

Yes. What would make this barbecue perfect for him would be Amber at his side.

THE NEXT DAY spectators poured into the fields and pastures of the Beaumont Ranch, and Amber was one of them. Beaumont High seniors parked the cars and asked for a donation of five dollars for the ambulance fund.

She noticed a line at Smokin' Sammy's; the Boy and Girl Scouts' hot dog and burger booth was just as crowded. So was the pizza booth that the Elks Lodge operated.

The bull riders were signing autographs in the arena. They were all dressed in their vests, which were loaded with sponsor patches, jeans, chaps, long-sleeved shirts, hats, boots and the biggest belt buckles known to exist.

The arena announcers were going to be the Beaumont brothers. They would take turns when they weren't riding.

Amber had planned her entrance into the arena when Jesse was about to announce Luke's ride on White Whale.

"Jesse, sorry I'm late, but I can take over now," Amber said. Jesse looked confused but relieved that he could concentrate on his own riding.

"Ladies and gentlemen, in chute number four, wearing number one on his vest, is Luke Beaumont, last year's Professional Bull Riders world champion. Luke is on White Whale, who happens to be last year's Bull of the Year. This is going to be quite a match-up."

The chute gate opened and White Whale came charging out. He immediately went right and spun like a top while jumping at the same time. Luke hung on, matching White Whale jump for jump. The crowd went wild and were on their feet cheering for Luke.

Amber held her breath as she always did when he rode. This time she held it for eight seconds. The buzzer rang and Luke jumped off, but he got hung up with his hand in the rigging.

The three volunteer bull fighters pulled at his rope, but White Whale kept bucking. Luke was in danger of being stomped. Amber heard screams in the arena but hers was the loudest, as Luke tried to stay on his feet and not go underneath the bull.

Finally, Luke's hand came out of his rigging.

Amber let out her breath as Luke ran to the fence and climbed it so White Whale wouldn't hunt him down and roll him like a log.

Then Amber realized that she should be talking about Luke's ride…after all, she was the arena announcer.

"Ladies and gentleman, the scores are coming in for Luke's ride. That was a 92-point ride! What do you think about Luke Beaumont riding the Bull of the Year? Let's hear it!"

The stands exploded with hoots and yeehaws. Someone brought a confetti cannon and tiny pieces of colored paper rained down on Luke.

LUKE WALKED TOWARD Amber with a big grin. He took the microphone from her hand, gave it to some tech guy and lifted her over the fence onto the arena dirt because he wanted the whole of Beaumont to know that she was his.

He gave her a big hug and kiss as the crowd went wild.

"Thanks for coming back, Amber."

But Luke didn't realize until three seconds later that he'd forgotten one of the important rules of bull riding: make sure the bull you just rode was out of the arena and fenced in the back before you let your guard down.

White Whale was on the loose.

Luke was so happy to see Amber, he forgot about the rule; he didn't think.

He'd just put the woman he loved in danger. Was he insane?

The crowd screamed as he pushed Amber to the fence surrounding the arena. "Climb, Amber!"

The bull came charging toward Luke. He executed a duck and a dodge that led the bull away from Amber until the arena bull fighters could get the animal in the back and the fence locked shut behind him.

Luke jogged toward the announcer's booth. "Amber, I'm so damned sorry."

"Luke, no problem. I'm fine. Actually, it was exhilarating. Like the rush I get when I capture a criminal. I can see why you like riding."

"Come with me." He took her hand and they walked out of the arena.

"Amber, it's great to see you!" He hugged her close to his body. "But what are you doing here?"

"It's a long story, Luke. No. I take that back. It's a short story. I was a big fish in a small pond here. Over there, I was a guppy. And they were very formal and acted like they were on active military duty. Which is okay, but it wasn't for me. It just wasn't what I thought. But most of all, I missed you."

Kiss me, Luke!

He teased her lips with his tongue. She opened for him and kissed him with all the love in her heart.

"Amber, after the rodeo is over, let's talk. We'll go in the ranch house, but if my father is leading tours, we'll talk in the barn. Meet you there."

"Got it."

It was good to hear that Big Dan Beaumont was out of rehab and back at the ranch. Amber went back to announcing. The bull riding was exciting and the riders were top-notch. She felt confident talking about each rider, since she had a day sheet that one of the Beaumonts must have compiled. Another sheet had pertinent stats that she used extensively. She was on a roll.

The spectators were excited and cheering for all the riders, standing on their feet when it seemed like a bull rider was injured. EMTs were standing by along with the decrepit ambulance and Donny Cushman's hearse. At least Donny had had enough sense to park the hearse out of sight.

After the bull riding was over, Amber was glad to turn the microphone over to her replacement, Dwight Frenza. Dwight was the arena announcer for rodeos and bull ridings far and wide.

Now it was time for the amateurs to show their stuff. The bronc riding was next, with fifteen entrants. They all rocked their broncs and all made eight seconds.

The steer wrestling had sixteen entrants. They were big, tough-looking guys who could jump off their horses and wrestle a steer to the ground. The winner got the job done in 4.82 seconds.

The rodeo ended and Dwight announced that the riders would be in the arena signing autographs and that Smokin' Sammy's House of Hickory would be serving until dark.

The event was a total success and Amber couldn't have been happier. It pulled the town together, just like it had in the past, when everyone used to look forward to the annual Beaumont Ranch Rodeo. She couldn't wait until all the receipts were in to see how close they were to buying an ambulance.

Amber walked up the path to the ranch house, anticipating how it would look after all the work was done.

But she stopped walking and stared at her family's modified stock truck. It had a huge sign on the front proclaiming Chapman's Craft Distilled Liquors. Now, her father's moonshine had flavors like mango-banana and pumpkin-coconut.

Cautiously, she approached the truck. There were jars stacked from floor to ceiling.

"Uh… Dad, this is quite the operation. So this is the reason for all the jars in your living room! I don't suppose you are legal, are you?"

"You betcha, Amber. Totally legal. I have a license from the state. Remember when you were directing traffic? I was picking up my license. We are a legal operation, and our fruity moonshine—I mean, distilled liquor—is selling like hotcakes!"

"Yeehaw! I was so worried that you were going back to moonshining, but in a way you have! But you're legal this time. Good for you, Dad!"

"Thanks, Amber." They hugged for a while, and then her father cleared his throat and whispered in her ear.

"And we have a lot of requests for pomegranate. I just have to figure out what a pomegranate is." He laughed then moved her away to look into her eyes. "Amber, are you here to stay?"

"Yes. Yes, I am." She gave her father a big hug and a kiss on the cheek. "I'm moving into my old apartment over the Happy Tea Pot."

"I'm glad you're back. We missed you. And your mother is here, too. Your three brothers and I cleaned all the junk out, painted the house and your mother picked out new furniture. Then she moved in. So, my whole family is here in Beaumont. Life is good."

"Yes, Dad. Life is good, but I have a feeling that it's going to be much better."

THERE WAS A line waiting to get into the ranch house for a Big Dan tour, so Amber went to the barn. What a difference from the decaying, moldering structure to the bright, sweet-smelling building that it was now.

The temporary shed that Luke had built was now enclosed. It contained tack and was stocked with hay, oats, grain and vitamins and other supplies.

"You did a wonderful job on the bull riding, Amber," Luke said, slipping his arm around her waist. "I never knew you could announce like that."

"In case I need a new career, I know what to do. But the barn is incredible. What a difference!"

"I owe it all to you, you know." He bent his head and kissed her. "Thanks so much everything," he whispered in her ear then nibbled on her neck.

"It looks like we made enough money for a new ambulance and a fire truck, but the jury is still out. We might be able to squeeze another ambulance in."

Luke took her hands in his and kissed her palms. "What a terrific event. I'm running out of ways to describe it."

"Awesome. Awesome covers everything."

"Amber, are you going to go back to your old job?"

"I talked to Fitz. Yes. I'm going back to my old job. Then I'm going to take a leave of absence and do some traveling. Know anyone who travels...say, on the Professional Bull Riders circuit?"

He pulled her toward him and kissed the tip of her nose. "It just so happens that I know a bull rider who'd love a traveling partner."

"Just a traveling partner?" she asked.

"Hell, no. She'll be a good friend, someone who I can talk to, and someone who loves Beaumont, Oklahoma, as much as I do."

"What about *Luke* Beaumont?" Amber asked. "I know someone who has had a crush on Luke Beaumont since grammar school. And she loves him."

"And I love her." He kissed her hard, passionate, and Amber hoped he'd never let her go.

Epilogue

"You did it, Luke!" Amber whispered in Luke's ear as they stood in front of the chutes in the huge arena for the big award presentation. "Good for you."

"Since we've been traveling together, you've brought me good luck."

"Good to know."

"How many?" he whispered in her ear.

"How many what?" she asked, puzzled.

"Children. Remember when we talked about children, and you said that you'd like six. How about three girls and three boys?"

She laughed. "Yes! But I was thinking of six and six."

"That works for me, but we'd better get busy."

"I'll do my part," she whispered back. She smiled. "That's what I've always been sad about. I thought I'd never have any kids."

The department had an excellent maternity leave plan, and she could always change her shift or work part-time. They'd work out the details later.

He grinned. "I'll do my part, too."

The TV announcer, Mia Jackson, arrived at Luke's side. "Luke Beaumont. Two back-to-back wins! What an accomplishment! Will we see you next season, Luke?"

"No, you won't, Mia. I'm going to retire. I have plans on expanding the Beaumont Ranch, and Amber and I plan on becoming contractors and hope to supply a lot of rough stock for the PBR. I'm also going to run a rodeo school on the grounds."

"Sounds great, Luke, but we'll miss watching you ride. And now for the gold buckle presentation."

The CEO of the PBR handed Luke his gold buckle. "Congratulations, Luke."

Just then, Luke went down on one knee in front of everyone at the arena. "Amber, I love you. Will you marry me?"

Excitement bubbled up inside of her. This was like some beautiful dream. She could see her whole happy future ahead of her and a house full of laughter and happiness with Luke.

"I thought you'd never ask! Of course I'll marry you!" She pulled him off the ground and gave him a big kiss.

"Ladies and gentlemen, the lady said yes!" Mia said.

The applause was deafening.

"Amber, I don't have a ring right now, but will this gold buckle do?"

"Of course!" She kissed him and whispered in his ear, "Luke, you've always been my gold buckle cowboy!"

* * * * *

If you loved this story, don't miss
Christine Wenger's other books:

THE RANCHER'S SURPRISE SON
LASSOED INTO MARRIAGE
HOW TO LASSO A COWBOY
THE COWBOY CODE
THE TYCOON'S PERFECT MATCH
IT'S THAT TIME OF YEAR
THE COWBOY AND THE CEO
NOT YOUR AVERAGE COWBOY
THE COWBOY WAY

All available now from Harlequin Special Edition!

Get 2 Free Books,

HARLEQUIN®
Western Romance

Plus 2 Free Gifts—

just for trying the Reader Service!

SPECIAL EXCERPT FROM

H **HARLEQUIN**®
™

Western Romance

*Cole McCullough must find the birth mother of the
twin babies left outside his door. When his ex-girlfriend
Stacy Rowe offers to help, he's in for much more than he
bargained for!*

*Read on for a sneak preview of
the next heartwarming installment of the
FOREVER, TEXAS series,
TWINS ON THE DOORSTEP,
by USA TODAY bestselling author Marie Ferrarella!*

"You really found these babies on your doorstep?" Stacy
asked several minutes later.

She had gotten into the back seat of his truck and he had
handed her the wicker basket with the babies. The infants
were dozing and the silence in the truck felt overwhelming.
Stacy couldn't think of anything else to say, and every
other topic would set them off on a course she had no
desire to travel.

"Yes, I did," he answered, getting into the driver's seat.
He glanced at her over his shoulder.

As if she didn't know where he'd found the babies, he
thought.

He was staring at her, Stacy realized, and it took
everything she had not to squirm in her seat. This was a
totally bad idea, going with Cole to the clinic like this. But
no one said no to Miss Joan, and Stacy wasn't about to be
the first. She had no desire to have her head handed to her.

"Do you have any idea who the mother might be?" Stacy asked him.

Okay, Cole thought, he'd play along. "There might be a few possibilities," he responded vaguely. "But that's why I came with them to Miss Joan. She's always on top of everything and I figure that she'd be the first to know whose babies they were."

"Miss Joan doesn't know everything," Stacy insisted.

"Maybe," he agreed. "But right now, I figured she was my best shot."

Why are we playing these games, Stacy? Tell me the truth. Are these babies mine?

For one moment, he wrestled with an overwhelming desire to ask the woman in the back seat just that. It would explain why she'd left town so abruptly. But he knew asking her was pointless. He knew her. She wouldn't answer him. In all likelihood, she'd just walk out on him the way she had the last time.

And, angry as he was about her leaving him, he didn't want that happening again. Not until he'd had a chance to talk with her—*really* talk.

Don't miss TWINS ON THE DOORSTEP
by Marie Ferrarella, available October 2017
wherever Harlequin® Western Romance books
and ebooks are sold.

www.Harlequin.com

LOVE
Harlequin
romance?

Join our Harlequin community to share your thoughts and connect with other romance readers!

Be the first to find out about promotions, news, and exclusive content!

Sign up for the Harlequin e-newsletter and download a free book from any series at

www.TryHarlequin.com

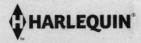

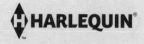